How Could Michael Possibly Think Of Himself As A Failure With Women?

He was a woman's dream of a man: honest, warm, a caretaker and protector by nature, a man who empathized and listened and cared. Simone just couldn't climb into her car and disappear without somehow showing him that she thought he was damn special.

It was just another impulse, that she bounced up on tiptoe and brushed his cheek. It was meant to be a peck. A gesture of affection. Nothing more. Nothing that should have ignited a maelstrom.

But he turned his head at just that moment, so her lips didn't land on his cheek. They landed on his mouth. In that speck of a second when they were both surprised, the contact had the same dangerous effect as instant glue.

They were already...fused.

Dear Reader,

Just when you thought Mother Nature had turned up the heat, along comes Silhouette Desire to make things even *hotter*. It's June...the days are longer, the kids are out of school, and we've got the very best that romance has to offer.

Let's start with our *Man of the Month, Haven's Call*, which is by Robin Elliott, a writer many of you have written to tell me is one of your favorites.

Next, we have *Salty and Felicia* by Lass Small. If you've ever wondered how those two older Browns got together, well, now you'll get to find out! From Jennifer Greene comes the latest installment in her JOCK'S BOYS series, *Bewildered*. And Suzanne Simms's series, HAZARDS, INC., continues with *The Pirate Princess*.

Anne Marie Winston has created a tender, wonderful story, *Substitute Wife*. And if you like drama and intensity with your romance, don't miss Lucy Gordon's *Uncaged!*

It just doesn't get any better than this...so read and enjoy.

All the best,

Lucia Macro
Senior Editor

Please address questions and book requests to:
Reader Service
U.S.: P.O. Box 1325, Buffalo, NY 14269
Canadian: P.O. Box 1050, Niagara Falls, Ont. L2E 7G7

JENNIFER GREENE
BEWILDERED

SILHOUETTE *Desire*®
Published by Silhouette Books
America's Publisher of Contemporary Romance

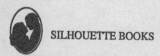

SILHOUETTE BOOKS

ISBN 0-373-05861-6

BEWILDERED

Copyright © 1994 by Jennifer Greene

JENNIFER GREENE

lives near Lake Michigan with her husband and two children. Before writing full-time, she worked as a personnel manager, teacher and college counselor. Michigan State University honored her as an "outstanding woman graduate" for her work with women on campus.

Ms. Greene has written over thirty-five category romances for which she has won many awards, including the Rita for "Best Short Contemporary" book from Romance Writers of America and "Best Series Author" from *Romantic Times*.

To Lucia—
For all your patience, perception and understanding, I
owe you a mountain of thanks. I haven't a clue how I
had the incomparable good luck to find you for an
editor...but I'm glad I did.
I wish you all the best.

Prologue

Well, there was clearly no rest for the wicked. The sound of a slammed door, three stories below, woke Jock from the best erotic dream he'd had in a century. Feeling aggravated, he climbed out of bed and pressed his nose to the window.

It was dark outside. Clouds covered the full moon, and the wind was whipping up a storm. The pitchy night was almost as dark as the sleek, satin-black car in the driveway. The vehicle had to belong to the third Connor brother—Michael—but Jock couldn't catch a look at him. The open car trunk blocked his view. A leather suitcase appeared on the driveway, then another, then a case for one of those twentieth-century computer contraptions, then more of the paraphernalia that went with those silly things. Finally the trunk door closed.

Jock squinted hard as he snared his first glance at the lad. Lar, what was he going to do with this one? 'Twas true the other two Connor brothers had made his life a living hell, but the result was all that mattered. He'd successfully managed both of them. He'd hoped, though—he'd really hoped—that Michael would turn out to be an easier project.

It didn't look that way. Even accounting for the unfamiliar styles, Jock could still recognize a hand-tailored suit, shoes with a spit shine and the kind of clothing that reeked of pricey. He'd never get on with a blooming aristocrat. Couldn't read himself, never saw any reason to waste his time on anything so foolish as book learning. The lad not only looked smart, but the way he stood, the way he moved, reflected a man of power and command, a leader type comfortable with authority. Rats.

Jock squinted harder, determined to find something positive about the situation. And he did. The lad was moving fast, trying to move all his gear and paraphernalia under cover, but the wind was riffling through his hair. Thick hair, darkish blond. He wore spectacles, but that wasn't all bad. Spectacles were easily broken. He was built more elegant than brawny—regrettable, for sure—but Jock suspected that leanness was misleading. He had the height and breadth of shoulder to protect a woman. More relevant to the lasses, the lad was a looker. Even the dim light revealed a good nose, a strong chin, high cheekbones, easily the kind of face to make a woman's heart flutter. He had some age on him. Late thirties? And he wasn't the type to walk in anyone's shadow. A man's pride was mirrored in his face, the lines of experience and character honed in his profile.

Jock heaved a sigh. A proudful man could be a trial, and for sure they'd have a bit of trouble relating. Jock communicated best in a brawl or over a mug of rum; men of class and power were a wee bit out of his realm. Still, he'd never feared a challenge. At an elemental level, there wasn't a man born who wasn't motivated by loneliness and sex. Most men felt uncomfortable talking about love—Jock could well comprehend that—but in the darkest nights, in the bleakest moments in a man's life, there was only one thing that could sustain a man's soul.

Abruptly Jock's mood lifted. He'd found a way to handle the other brothers, hadn't he? This one could hardly be more difficult. It was simply a matter of putting the right woman directly in his path. If nature failed to take her course, there was always the option of throwing in a ghostly machination or two. Jock knew his business. The whole project was going to be—in the silly slang of the day—a piece of cake. The lad would never know what hit him.

From the moment Michael Connor crossed the threshold, he was one of Jock's boys.

One

Ignoring the spit of rain and the howling wind, Michael Connor took a long look around the yard. The For Sale sign was up, the real estate firm and telephone number clearly printed. As it should be. The grass was freshly mowed, the grounds spotless. He'd ordered that job done, too.

After slamming the trunk of his car, he grabbed his computer case. It took two trips to cart all his gear to the shelter of the front porch. A witch's brew of a summer storm was coming in. Roiling clouds clustered over the Atlantic; waves pounded on the wild, bouldery shore; lightning crackled in the distance. A romantic might find the view captivating.

Michael dug into his suit pocket for the house key. If he had a choice, he'd put the view in a trash bin. The same went for the house, and yeah, he'd glanced at her. She was built in the time of clipper ships and Revolutionary War pirates, a sprawling, three-story structure with a castle-like turret at one corner and a widow's walk wrapped around her top floor. Lots of character. Lots of charm. Michael couldn't wait to get rid of her.

So far, both his younger brothers had tried. Like a pesky mosquito—or a used car salesman—the nuisance refused to go away. The Maine coastal property was obviously a prize nugget of real estate. At the right price, even in recession times, she should sell faster than a finger snap. Yet from the time their grandfather had willed them the old monster, the damn house had stuck to the Connor men like a clinging mistress who just wouldn't let go.

That, of course, was about to change. Michael had the ball now.

He clipped up the porch steps. Lightning flashed, momentarily lighting the whole house with an eerie, ghostly glow. He ignored it. Zachary and Seth had both warned him that there was something mystical—even magical—about the place. Michael found that warning humorous. There was only reason the house hadn't been sold. It had nothing to do with magic. Both his brothers had simply been blindsided and sidetracked by the advent of women in their lives.

Truthfully, Michael didn't mind being left the problem of the house. Problems such as this were easy, an annoying waste of time but nothing he couldn't handle in his sleep, and his brothers' happiness mattered far more. Both weddings had been a relief, the brides a source of joy. The Connor men had a long, painful history of bad luck with women. Ironically it used to chafe Michael that he was the only one who'd successfully broken that pattern. For ten years he'd been married, as snug as a bug in a rug, a role model—he'd hoped—for the younger brothers he'd helped raise.

The ink on the divorce decree was long dry, but the failure of his marriage still stung, still gnawed on his mind. He'd never failed at anything. Not soccer, not poker, not school or business, and certainly, nothing that had ever critically mattered to him. Quickly, he smothered that train of thought before the engine could rev up. Thinking about Carla only sent acid shooting to his stomach.

He jammed the key into the old-fashioned lock. The heavy oak door swung open with an eerie creak. Before his hand could locate a light switch, he heard a telephone ringing from somewhere in the depths of the house.

He found the switch. A chandelier suddenly glared with wincing brightness, illuminating a two-landing staircase and a wainscotted hall with a maze of rooms on both sides. There were no phones in sight, but it wasn't hard to track the nearest jangling sound to the kitchen on the far left. He reached the old-fashioned wall receiver before the fourth ring.

"Mr. Connor? This is Paula Stanford. I was hoping to catch you tonight, but I wasn't sure what time you planned to arrive."

Michael crooked the receiver between his ear and shoulder, relaxing as he loosened his tie. Stanford was the name of the real estate agent. He'd talked to her on the phone before. Technically he could have passed the sale of the property on to her—if he was prepared to trust anyone but himself. He wasn't. The albatross of a house had been a thorn in his side for too long now. As Michael knew well, if a man wanted something seriously done, he'd better take total control of the cards.

"I could meet with you tomorrow, if you wanted. Just name the time."

Michael did. Ten o'clock, sharp. Mentally he'd already pictured Ms. Stanford. Brunette, buxom, mid-fifties, a little plump. Her tone was deferential; maybe she'd researched enough of his background to know he had money. Something in her voice made him think of dime-store perfume.

It was a game he played, figuring out people solely from their voice on the telephone. His scorecard with men was ten out of ten. With women, it was more like four—an aggravating measure of how little he understood the female of the species, but hardly a surprise, considering how totally he'd misread his own wife. Still, he didn't have to understand Ms. Stanford to work with her. So far she'd followed his instructions to the letter. They were going to get along just fine.

Once he hung up the receiver, he hustled back outside for the rest of his gear. The spit of rain had turned into a deluge of a sludging downpour. Thunder growled in the darkness, just as he kicked the door closed—and the telephone rang again.

No question he needed his answering machine and fax hooked up before the night was over. This time, he snatched the receiver before the third ring. "Mr. Connor? This is Sam Burkholtz at the plant."

Michael finished pulling off his tie and folded it neatly on the counter as he listened. He had two die-cast operations in Detroit. The first shift production staff could walk into engineering or maintenance if they had a problem. Because the second and third shifts had less support staff, they had instructions to call him directly if there was a problem. Sam's voice radiated nervousness. He was new, and undoubtedly didn't believe that the boss didn't mind being called at any hour of the day or night. He'd learn, eventually, that nothing aggravated Michael—except finding out about a problem too late to do anything about it. Whether he was in Timbuktu or Maine made no difference. He kept control.

He'd hung up and made it as far as the door, when the telephone jangled yet again. This call, though, made him laugh.

Both twins demanded equal time on the line. Davie had scored a hit in a Little League game. Michael listened to the blow-by-blow—twice—and then Donnie yanked the receiver and described the action all over again. His nine-year-old sons were the hands-down joy of his life. They seemed to be doing okay with the split up, but putting them through the divorce still yanked on his conscience. He'd have stayed in the worst marriage on earth for their sakes. Carla hadn't made that a choice—in fact, she'd made it blisteringly clear that she couldn't stand to even be around him.

It had been a crippling blow and a shock—blindly believing himself to be a good guy one day, discovering the next that he was as repulsive as a dead skunk. Thankfully he had sons and not daughters. Boys, he understood.

" ... Yeah, yeah, I told you. If I'm here more than three weeks, I promise you can fly up and stay with me. With any luck, though, I'll be home long before then. What I'm doing here is nothing but boring, trust me. How're the swimming lessons going?"

Michael should have known better than to ask the question. Both monsters claimed dolphin blood and Olympic swimming skills. Davie had had a scare in a swimming pool the year before. He'd revolted at the idea of swimming lessons, didn't want to get near water again and his clone—no surprise—backed him up. Michael didn't take a hard line with the kids often, but the near drowning had terrified him. Both boys had conveniently forgotten how hard they'd fought against the lessons. Naturally. They had a new agenda.

"We're so good that we think you should put in a pool for us, Dad," Donnie suggested. Davie echoed his enthusiasm.

Michael heard out their sales pitch, and finally said, "Maybe." A chorus of groans expressed what they thought of *that* parental tactic. A few minutes later, still chuckling, he hung up the phone.

His smile slowly faded. The house was suddenly silent, too silent. Unfamiliar. Alien. Lonely. He wasn't looking forward to the long night ahead. Shrugging out of his suit coat, he draped the jacket over a chair and rolled his shoulders. His eyes burned from tiredness. Normally he had energy to burn, but he hadn't slept well in months now. From the time he was knee high, he'd been a chronic insomniac. Marriage had solved the problem, but with Carla gone, it was back with a vengeance.

The wry thought crossed his mind that there should be a rent-a-body service in the Yellow Pages. The failure of his marriage had made him acutely aware that he didn't understand women. He didn't want to put another one through torture. But he'd pay an unbelievably high fee not to have to sleep alone. He wouldn't care if she stole the covers. He wouldn't care if she spoke a single word. He'd even willingly put a dead bolt on his frustrated libido. All he wanted was a living, breathing, female body to wrap himself around during the night.

Somewhere, he heard a clock ticking. Rain sluiced down the kitchen windows in silver streaks. A strange draft of cold air brushed past him, startling him, then making him shake his head impatiently. Naturally an old house had drafts and shadows. It wasn't like him to be spooked. The place was just so yawning big and empty.

He forced himself to move. There was a flask of Scotch in his shaving-kit case. He found a water glass, poured the Chivas, and carried it around as he settled in. The Scotch wouldn't cure his restlessness, couldn't begin to dent his insomnia, but sometimes it blurred the edges of the loneliness. Switching lights on and off, he checked out the downstairs rooms. One was apparently a library—the three walls of bookshelves were empty—but there was a desk, and tall windows overlooking the ocean view. He stashed his computer and electronic equipment in there, then headed back to the front hall for his luggage.

As he reached the upstairs landing with his leather cases, the telephone rang yet again. The sound was close, so there was definitely a receiver on the second floor; he just had no idea which bedroom it was in. There were at least a half-dozen doors to choose from. When the phone jangled again, he picked up the trail, stumbling through a doorway and groping in the dark for the receiver on a bedside table.

"Mr. Connor? Michael Connor?"

"You got him." Blindly his fingers connected with the ceramic shape of a lamp, but he almost knocked it over trying to find the switch. Even distracted, though, the caller's voice pricked his curiosity. None of the calls he'd received so far had been totally unexpected. This one was.

There was no reason an unfamiliar woman should have wanted him—much less gone to the trouble of hunting him down here. The voice was a little breathless, a little nervous, pitched low, a molasses-soft alto. The game was so automatic that he didn't even think about it. His mind started making pictures. Brown-haired, brown-eyed, plain. Mid-twenties. Still definitively young, small in size, real short hair and the kind to use something sweet and flowery for a scent. Clothes, buttoned up to the neck. Little print stuff. Skirts that covered her knees. A real shy type.

"...I'm terribly sorry to bother you. I know you don't know me. My name is Simone Hartman." She hesitated. "I don't suppose there's a prayer that rings a bell for you?"

"Sorry. No." He almost added a "honey," then checked himself. His sixty-year-old secretary, Roberta, had recently schooled him in all the taboos related to sexual harassment. Roberta claimed that even a Neanderthal could learn. You should never tell a female employee she looked nice; she could get the horrifying idea that you'd looked below her neck. You never patted a woman on the back, no matter how terrific a job she'd done. You never raised your voice, because when he raised his voice, Roberta claimed he scared the women to death. And you sure as hell never called a woman "honey"—even if she did sound like a vulnerable waif. "Should I know the name? Do we have some connection?"

"It was possible you'd know. Because, yes, we have a connection, a personal connection, but... darn, this is so hard to explain over the phone. I just didn't know how to contact you. I called the real estate number on the sign, but no one would give me your phone number—at least the phone number where you lived. The best the woman would tell me was that you were due to arrive in town this week, hopefully by today."

"Okay. Well, you've got me now. I still don't know what you want." Michael figured the chances of their having a "personal connection" were about five million to one. If he'd heard that molasses-soft voice before, he would have remembered it. Something fringy tangled around his fingers. He was still wrestling with the lamp. So far the score was three for the lamp, and zero for him. The room was pitch-dark, the wind shrieking through every crack, and Michael was fast losing patience with the conversation, the house, and for sure, the damn lamp.

"My connection is with your grandfather. The man who bought the house around the Depression time in the thirties? I haven't got the wrong family, do I? You are related to Benjamin Connor?"

The lamp blinked on at the same instant she mentioned his grandfather's name. It was unfortunate timing. Michael's jaw dropped at his first glimpse of the master bedroom. Both his brothers had mentioned the room was "something else," but he sure hadn't been expecting a hooker's lair. Holy spit. The Victorian fringed lamp only cast a wavering light, hardly denting the shadowed corners, but he could still see the red velvet drapes and lounging settee and the pedestal bed big enough for a sultan—and an ample-size harem.

"Mr. Connor, are you there?"

"Yeah, I'm here."

"And Benjamin Connor was your grandfather?"

"Yes." Not that he was thrilled to admit the blood tie, Michael thought dryly. He washed a hand over his face, disbelieving the old reprobate's choice in decor.

"Thank heavens," she murmured. "Mr. Connor, if it's at all possible, I need to see you. Would it be possible for me to set up an appointment? I'm staying at a bed and breakfast in Bar Harbor, and the sole reason I'm here is to connect with you. It doesn't make any difference what day or time."

"Honey..." Aw hell, he'd said the forbidden word. "Ms. Hartman, I really don't understand. What's this about? How do you know about my grandfather? This house?"

She hesitated. "That's exactly what I want to tell you, but it just isn't something I can say on the phone."

She wouldn't budge from that rock. Michael swallowed a gulp of Scotch, and suspecting he was making a mistake, told her that he had an hour free at nine the next morning.

Once he hung up, he was exasperated with himself. He had little patience for the "can't tell you on the phone" ploy. People who refused to deal straight invariably weren't. When someone went to the trouble of tracking him down, they almost always wanted something from him. Michael was used to that, but he usually gave short thrift to anyone who didn't show their cards.

Her claim to a connection with his grandfather intrigued him, though. More to the point, it needled him.

He took another sip of Scotch, letting the smooth golden liquid roll on his tongue until it burned before swallowing. His hard gaze focused on the room again.

Michael didn't like mysteries, and there was more than one associated with his grandfather. The existence of this house was the first. No one in the family knew that Benjamin Connor even had this property until he died and left it to his three grandsons. Benjamin was from Colorado—nowhere near Maine. To the family's knowledge, he'd never had any ties in Maine.

Selling the white elephant was the only conceivable choice. None of the brothers wanted it; none lived anywhere near the area; it would be a monster to keep up and it wasn't as if the place had any sentimental value. Still, the question of how their grandfather had happened to own the property—what he did here— didn't seem to haunt Seth and Zach. It did Michael.

Benjamin was a larger-than-life legend in the Connor family. He'd been an orphan—the first of the clan—and he'd raised himself by his bootstraps to make a fortune in Colorado silver. That part of his life, Michael respected, but the old reprobate couldn't keep his hands off the ladies. Marriage hadn't stopped him from playing around—or flashing his mistresses in public. The macho-stud stories were recirculated every holiday, as if the old man's legendary tomcatting was something "real men" should admire. Michael had never seen it that way.

The Connor men's bad luck with women had started with the old man. Benjamin only had one son. Michael's dad. And it always struck Michael that if his father had known anything about love and loving—real love, real loving—his mother might have stuck around. Instead, she'd split, leaving three young sons in a motherless household. Michael had been the oldest, nine at the time. He'd always felt responsible for his brothers, always took care of them, but none of them had been exposed to a woman's influence. How were they supposed to know about women when there were none around? How were they supposed to know how to love, to relate to and care for a woman, when there was never a female in their sphere?

Michael rolled the last of the Scotch in his glass. More than once it had occurred to him that maybe there was a genetic flaw. Something missing in the Connor men, some mistake in their makeup, that mysterious something it took to really hold and keep a woman happy. His failure with Carla wasn't genetic. He'd screwed up. Royally. Totally. But the *how* still bewildered him.

In a thousand years, he'd never planned, never wanted, to turn out like his grandfather. The old coot had been a scoundrel. A user of women, a manipulative, selfish bastard. You couldn't choose your relatives, but Michael had grown up with a violent determination to be different than the old man. He thought he had—until Carla walked out. And his blood-tie to a man who notoriously failed with women became pretty damn hard to deny.

Maybe this Simone Hartman had some answers for him.

Maybe she didn't.

Michael suspected their meeting tomorrow would be a total waste of time, but if she actually had some information about his grandfather, he'd listen. Directly and indirectly, the old man had affected his life for too damn many years to cut off the chance to learn something about him.

The thought of meeting her actually made him smile. He'd studiously—religiously—avoided the female of the species since his divorce, but Michael was hard-pressed to believe he needed to be careful around Simone. Her molasses-soft voice had been soothing, calming, sweet. There was just nothing there to arouse his masculine warning instincts.

Hell, even he could handle a waif.

Two

Brilliant sunshine poured through the narrow tall windows of the library. Michael had quit trying to sleep around 5:00 a.m. An unknown number of hours had passed since then. At the moment, he was sitting on the floor with his white sleeves rolled up, and he was about to go out of his mind.

He had a brilliant head for business. Anyone who knew him gave him credit for that. Hell, one of his competitors had nicknamed him Rumpelstiltskin, disgustedly claiming he could probably spin straw into gold. From the time he opened a watered-down lemonade stand at the vulnerable age of six, he'd been making money hand over fist. Never mind all his character flaws, Michael knew damn well he was a smart man. So how could this possibly be so hard?

Traveling with electronic equipment meant traveling

with the sidekick electric cords and cables. Temporarily twenty of them were strewn like snakes on the library floor. The computer, fax, printer, monitor, keyboard, modem and answering machines were all out of their boxes. He could run his business anywhere, as long as he had those connections, and the heavy work was all done. All they needed was hooking up. Any second now—any second—he was going to get order and control over the mess.

His fourth mug of coffee was cooling on the desk. He reached for it, so absorbed in the project that he didn't initially hear the pounding on the front door. Eventually the persistent rapping registered in his brain. Muttering at the interruption, a pale gray computer cable still gripped in his fist, he strode down the hall and yanked open the front door.

A green-eyed blonde stood on his porch. He didn't know her from Adam, but one glance reminded him why he'd had the brilliant good sense to choose a nice, safe, male-dominated business like die cast. He knew how to handle men. And even before Carla, there were certain women who made him want to tiptoe in the other direction, fast.

She was one of them.

There was nothing intimidating about her clothes. She apparently favored a conservative, tailored style—which he could certainly relate to. Her white slacks had a meticulous crease, a cinched-in belt, and molded demurely over noticeably plump hips. She'd paired the slacks with a square-necked top, rosish in color, that might have hinted at cleavage if she had any. The figure was pear-shaped and ordinary—but her face sure wasn't.

God, those eyes. Their color was a clear dark jade and framed with thick, soft lashes. Any man could get rattled looking into eyes that deep, that rich. She must have spent time in the sun, because her skin had the sun-brushed glow of a peach. Her face was oval-shaped and as striking as a cameo, fine-boned and elegant features, a straight nose, high cheekbones, delicately arched brows. Sensual. Everything about her was distinctly feminine and sensual. She wore no makeup except for a hint of gloss on her lips, but even her mouth looked softer than butter. Her hair tumbled in the ocean breeze, curling just to the drift of her shoulders, a streaky California gold in color and flyaway fine in texture. She wasn't overly tall. Maybe five foot seven? And not spring-young. About thirty, he guessed. Old enough to realize that her striking looks were always going to turn a man's head.

Michael could picture her paralyzing any number of men when she walked down the street; he could picture her sipping champagne in an expensive restaurant, but he sure as hell couldn't imagine what she was doing on his front porch.

"Mr. Connor? I called you yesterday? I'm Simone Hartman."

He stared at her blankly. It couldn't possibly be nine o'clock already, since he was never late for an appointment. And Simone Hartman was supposed to be brown-eyed, brown-haired and plain. A waif he could handle. He'd been so positive.

"May I come in?"

He closed his mouth. "Sure. I was expecting you." He caught the dance of humor in her eyes. Those damn eyes didn't miss much. His feet were bare, his hair disheveled and it was almost impossible to juggle the computer cable and tuck in his shirt at the same time. It wasn't like she looked him over head to toe in any blatant way, but her lips tipped in an impulsive smile.

"I obviously interrupted you right in the middle of something," she said. "Maybe I could help?"

"No, no. It's nothing I can't handle." He backed up to the parlor door and hurled the computer cable out of sight. It made a *thud* noise when it hit something. He smiled at her—his competent, full-of-authority, blue-suit smile. He could make a production staff of men jump with that particular smile. Her eyes just kept dancing. "I was going to get some coffee from the kitchen. Would you like a cup?"

"Sure. If it wouldn't be too much trouble."

She took a breath as she followed him down the hall. It was the first sign he'd noticed that she was nervous about meeting him, not nearly as confident as she seemed. And her voice was the same, molasses-soft and low; his masculine instincts had caught something vulnerable in that tone the night before and still did. It was just different, realizing that sweet voice was attached to an appallingly attractive woman. He stubbed his toe, rounding the corner into the kitchen. Where the *hell* were his shoes?

"I'd ask if you take cream and sugar, but I'm afraid I just got in last night. Temporarily I'm a little short on supplies."

"Black is fine. Mr. Connor—"

"Make it Michael." A little informality would surely ease this strange feeling of awkwardness. Smoothly he filched a cup from the cupboard, lifted the coffeepot from the stove and poured. A half cup of murky black liquid dribbled out. Heavily laden with dregs. He looked at those dancing green eyes, and sighed.

"I have a feeling it's not quite your morning," she murmured. "Really— I don't need the coffee anyway."

"Sure, you do. I'll make a fresh pot. It won't take long. Have a seat, and while you watch me bumble around here— I think I interrupted you a minute ago. You were about to say something?"

"Yes. I just wanted to tell you that I didn't mean to sound mysterious on the phone last night. It was just that what I had to tell you—and ask you—was frankly embarrassing."

Well, damn. She *was* nervous. The idea was so startling that he almost relaxed. "Interesting problem, but I hope you didn't lose any sleep over it. I'm thirty-six. You'd have to walk a long mile to say anything that would embarrass me." There now, he must have sounded reassuring because she smiled again. He rinsed out the pot and measured the cinnamon-vanilla ground beans. By some miracle, he didn't spill any. "You mentioned some tie to my grandfather?"

"Yes. No. Well…maybe the first thing I'd better tell you is that we're not related. We don't have any blood tie."

On a Richter scale, that hardly registered as a shock. Except for a few females passing through, the Connor family ran to all male relatives. If Michael had a ragtail cousin who looked like Simone, even if the relationship were forty times removed, he would definitely have noticed. "Something tells me this'll be easier for you if you just cut to the chase," he suggested dryly.

"Believe it or not, I'm trying to. I just wish there were some other way to say this but bluntly." She settled in a kitchen chair and cupped her chin in a palm. "My grandmother had an affair with your grandfather. She was married at the time. So, I believe, was he. This house was their 'place.' Where they met to... um...fool around.''

Michael turned his head, abruptly intrigued. He'd wondered for months how and why his grandfather had owned this house. His brothers were resigned that they'd never know the reason. "You're kidding? You know that for sure?''

"Positively. I only wish I didn't.'' Simone ruefully shook her head, the strands shimmering silver and gold where they caught the sun from the window. "I'm hardly proud to have to tell you that about my grandmother. Unfortunately when she was young, I don't think she had a moral in the cupboard. We've laughed about it—I mean, it's no disgrace to have a colorful relative in your past these days—but to be honest, I never thought her antics were all that funny. Her behavior had an enormous effect on the women in my family. Her bad judgment about life and men affected a lot of people—apparently your grandfather as well.''

Michael couldn't let that pass. "Maybe you'd better not be so quick to blame your grandmother. My grandfather was a classic scoundrel, more than capable of leading a woman down a garden path.''

By the time the fresh pot of coffee was done, he'd found his shoes and settled at the plank oak table across from her. She sat with a leg curled under her and her hands wrapped around a mug. When he first laid eyes on her, Michael would have bet the bank there wasn't a prayer of his feeling a kindred spirit camaraderie, ever, not with Simone.

But she talked the same language. Her grandmother sounded as selfish and irresponsible as his grandfather. The men in his family had all been affected by

Ben's choices; it sounded as if the women in her family had all been affected by Julia's. Simone had claimed on the telephone that the two of them had a personal tie. Who would have guessed that tie would turn out to be a matched pair of rapscallion relatives?

Who would have guessed that he'd been chuckling, bickering easily over whose relative was the worst reprobate, with a woman whose looks rattled every masculine nerve he'd ever had? Lord, her smile. Her mouth was small, soft, with the rouge tint of a rose. Her smile had a hint of wickedness, a hint of mischievousness— a grown woman's smile, definitely not a girl's—and her chuckle was as catching as chicken pox. Whoa there, he wanted to warn himself. Something was wrong. He never talked this easily or naturally with a woman he barely knew. He assumed it was the circumstances. It was pretty tough to feel distant or strange when the whole source of their conversation was the sex lives of their respectively embarrassing relatives.

"You've made this a hundred times easier to talk about than I expected," Simone said honestly. "But I'm afraid there's more. I haven't told you why I'm here."

"I figured you'd get to that eventually." He peered over, saw her mug was empty and lurched up to fetch the coffeepot again.

"I had no idea about this house or anything else until my grandmother told me about it, two weeks ago." At his questioning look, she nodded. "Yes, she's still alive. In a rest home now; she's really frail, and I'm afraid her heart is failing. In fact, I suspect that's the only reason she told me about her affair with your grandfather. Michael, she says she left some personal things in this house."

"Here?" Michael asked in surprise.

"Yes. I don't know why she would have left anything here. I don't know any details about the whole affair—like why or when they happened to break it off—but it apparently lasted a long time. Long enough for her to accumulate some personal mementos. Maybe they just didn't matter to her before. All I know is that she's beside herself now, afraid that she's going to die and these personal things are going to fall in the hands of strangers." Simone hesitated. "Look, I know I don't have any right to ask you. But I don't believe she's talking about anything of financial value. And nothing would calm her down until I agreed to fly up here and at least ask you if I could look around."

Michael gestured with a hand. "I don't have a problem with that. But I have to say—I just got here. I don't know what's here and what's not, but I've been in most of the rooms. There's some furniture, antiques. The kitchen had some dishes, but I haven't seen anything that looks like it would have any personal, sentimental meaning."

"Maybe there's a suitcase somewhere? Like in a closet, or an attic?" Simone sighed. "My grandmother's mind wanders in and out. It's more than possible that she sent me here on a wild-goose chase. If these things mattered so much to her, I don't know why in blazes she didn't take care of them years ago. But it's the only thing she ever asked me to do, and no matter what she's done, I love her. I know it's an intrusion and an imposition, and I don't want you thinking that I'm trying to rip off something that belonged to your grandfather—"

"Relax. I never thought any such..." The sound of someone pounding on the front door interrupted him.

Michael glanced at his watch with an impatient frown. "Damn. That's the real estate agent. This shouldn't take long, all right? I'll take care of her as quickly as I can."

"I don't want to be in your way—"

"You aren't. You won't be. I just have to handle this. We'll finish our talk as soon as she's gone."

The last thing Simone wanted to do was interrupt his business meeting, but it wasn't that easy to instantly disappear. Michael strode from the room before she could say anything else. Feeling awkward, she wrapped her arms around her chest and walked as far as the doorway, figuring that if she could see what was going on, she'd have a better idea if she should leave.

Her sense of humor was unexpectedly tickled, though, when Michael opened the front door. The woman who stepped into the hall was quite a piece of work. Apparently Michael had the same reaction, because he asked her name three times as if he'd been expecting someone else entirely.

Paula Stanford was dressed for success in a mustard linen suit, backless white heels and spangly crystal earrings. Her hair was a fascinating shade of red and the style framed her face in an artful, cascading froth of curls. The woman was pretty—honestly pretty, Simone thought—in spite of the fake lashes and face paint, and her baby blues certainly lit up like birthday candles when she laid eyes on Michael.

"Mr. Connor! I'm so delighted to finally meet you in person! We'll make it Michael and Paula, shall we? I feel like I already know you, and heaven knows, we're going to be working closely together."

Michael had his hand pumped. Fuchsia nails clutched his forearm affectionately. Ms. Stanford's eyes prowled the length of him as if she were an experienced butcher and he was the lushest piece of meat she'd ever seen. Simone took a sip of coffee, amused and bemused as she watched Michael shovel a hand through his hair.

He *had* to know the effect he had on women. His looks didn't matter to Simone—when she first walked in, the only thing on her mind was the uncomfortably insane mission she was on for her grandmother—but even so, how could she not notice? The thick brush of sandy hair. The long, elegant face, the strikingly brilliant blue eyes. He wasn't the kind of man to put on airs, but there was a quiet power in the way he held himself, perception and shrewd intelligence in his eyes, and energy—vital, virile male energy—in every movement he made.

His long lean body—his eyes, when he'd looked at her—had made her pulse thud. An annoying reaction. Very few men had made her pulse thud, and every time had been a prelude to disaster. Simone had learned the hard way to distrust her judgment about men. But she'd been so nervous when she walked in. Having to start a conversation about the intimacy of an illicit affair—sex—was *not* what she'd have chosen to do with a strange man. Worse yet, she'd obviously interrupted him right in the middle of some work project; there were smudged shadows under his eyes. He was obviously tired and harried.

Yet Michael had been both understanding and kind, and he'd made her laugh. By being so natural, he'd made her feel natural with him. Simone could handle herself—what woman of thirty-two hadn't learned to handle herself?—but she'd truly never expected to feel remotely comfortable around Michael Connor. She couldn't imagine anything throwing him.

Oddly enough, Ms. Paula Stanford seemed to be throwing him for six. Michael freed his hand and backed up a step. Ms. Stanford crowded a little closer. "Let's find some cozy place to sit," Paula cooed warmly. "It won't take us long to go through these papers. I think you'll be amazed at how efficiently I can handle everything for you."

Michael cleared his throat and said something polite. He backed up another step. Paula advanced again, her gaze rapt on his face. If Michael appreciated being looked at as if he were a Greek god, he should be having a terrific time.

"I assume you slept in the master bedroom last night. Isn't that room something? The first time I saw it, I'll tell you, I thought to myself that your grandfather must have been quite a stud. That room sure made me think of a fantasy or two." Paula winked.

Michael looked around wildly. To think he needed saving, Simone thought, was beyond ridiculous. He'd probably been handling women since he was knee-high.

Abruptly Ms. Stanford spotted her. Those heavily lashed eyes blinked real quickly, and the sugarcoating instantly disappeared from her tone. "And who's this? I'm sorry, I didn't realize anyone else was here. Somehow I had the impression that you weren't married and that you were traveling alone—"

"I'm not married—that is, I'm divorced—and I am traveling alone. This is—" Michael's gaze lanced her face.

In spite of the warm seventy-five degree morning, Simone felt the oddest cool draft at her back. There was obviously no unseen hand pushing her forward. It was just some silly reaction to stress. Still, since Michael seemed to be floundering, she finished his sentence for him. "I'm a friend of Michael's."

"A good friend," Michael qualified.

That was news to Simone, but now, she was stuck for an introduction. "Simone Hartman," she said as she ambled forward. Paula offered her a business-like handshake and a brilliant woman-to-woman smile. *I never meant to poach on your territory.* Lord. Talk about awkward. "Nice to meet you, Paula. Listen, I don't want to be in either of your way. You both want to talk about real estate business. Michael, I could come back later—"

His long, slim fingers closed on her wrist. Elegant hands, but the man had a grip like a vise. "You don't need to go. Really, this won't take long, will it, Ms. Stanford?"

It took forever.

They settled in the first room off the hall, an old-fashioned parlor with a tall stone fireplace and French doors leading down a long sloping lawn to the beach-front. The room was stocked with oversize, over-stuffed furniture from another era. Ms. Stanford spread a briefcase full of papers on the coffee table. Simone had no idea how she ended up on the rose damask horsehair couch, wedged between them. She had even less idea what on earth she was doing here.

Michael's long, muscular thigh pressed intimately against hers. It wasn't something she could ignore. His body was warm, electric with energy, and they were glued closer than lovers. Simone couldn't remember ever feeling this intense sexual awareness of a man. She'd be mortified if he knew, yet felt both thankful and confounded that it obviously wasn't going to be a problem.

As soon as Michael started talking business, he seemed to forget she was there. He never needed her as a buffer between him and Ms. Stanford. He didn't need anyone. Good grief, the man was a born steamroller. He automatically took control of the conversation, his tone brisk with authority. He clearly knew what he was doing, knew what he wanted and showed no doubt that he was going to get it.

"A hundred thousand asking price," he said curtly.

"Michael, as I've told you, the property is worth three times that," Ms. Stanford said unhappily. "Even that's low, and I'm sure I can find customers at that price. There's no reason for you to have go down, even in a buyer's market, not at this point—"

"The reason is that I want this property sold within a month. Money is secondary. I need this whole problem off my back. I want potential buyers in this house within days. I want it pushed. Hard and fast. I want it *gone*. If you can't handle that—"

"I can," Paula assured him swiftly.

They pushed papers, talked real estate-eze, discussed "points" and terms that might as well have been Greek to Simone. She wasn't bored. Watching Michael in action was like experiencing a 747 takeoff from the cockpit. All that power and command was right under his fingertips; he seemed to take it for granted. But it felt like forever before he finally stood up, Paula collected all her papers, and he ushered her out the front door.

When he came back, the hard-nosed business persona had disappeared. He stood in the doorway, rubbing the back of his neck. His gaze lanced her face again with a rueful expression. "Simone... I owe you big. I swear I didn't think it was going to take that long, and I'm real sorry you were stuck sitting through that. I know this is going to sound ridiculous—I'm sure I was imagining it—but I had the strangest feeling that woman was coming on to me."

"Ah... Michael?"

"What?"

"She was coming on to you with all the subtlety of a freight train." Simone added firmly, "She's a very pretty woman."

His eyebrows arched in thick wings. "Who could tell? Her perfume was so thick that it was hard to see her through the fog. And she sure wouldn't need a weapon in a dark alley. Did you notice those nails?"

Simone had to chuckle. "Come on. She was nice. She was just making her interest known."

"Yeah? Well, I'll give her due respect as a go-getter... especially if she applies that same kind of aggressiveness to selling the house," he said dryly. "In the meantime, I owe you."

She shook her head as she stood up. "You don't owe me anything."

"You stuck around and saved me from the vulture. I owe you, and I always pay my debts. You want diamonds, rubies, dinner?"

Simone wondered if he realized how naturally and easily he was teasing her—as if he already knew her, as if they somehow already understood each other. Abruptly she felt a vulnerable clutch of fear, a primitive instinct that Michael Connor was dangerous to her, too attractive, too interesting, a man of compelling deep waters when Lord, she knew better than to trust that kind of chemistry. "I never needed rubies and you don't have to spring for dinner," she said quickly. "All I'd like—if it's okay with you—is a chance to look for my grandmother's things."

"I thought we'd already settled that. You're welcome to look around—right now, if you have the time. Consider the house yours." He glanced at the library door. "I don't want to be rude, but there's some things I have to do. It's not like I could help you— I'm as unfamiliar with the house as you are. But there's nothing personal here of mine or my brothers. Feel free to poke in drawers or closets or wherever you want."

"It shouldn't take me long."

"I'm sure it won't."

Simone hesitated. "I still feel strange about this. For one thing, you don't have any reason to trust me. But I promise you that I'll show you anything that I find. I wouldn't take anything without asking you."

"Simone, I'm not worried that you're a thief," he said dryly. "Frankly I hope you come up with something, and I know darn well that my brothers would feel the same way. I'm curious about this affair our grandparents had."

"So am I." An understatement, Simone thought. She was more than curious about her grandmother's past. She was downright worried about what she was going to find. But that was nothing she could admit to Michael—or any other man.

Three

It was hard telling how long Simone would take exploring the house. An hour? Maybe two? Not that it made any difference to Michael. He headed straight for the library, propped his glasses on his nose and settled down to battle with the computer cables and electric cords again.

The telephone interrupted him several times. All were business, except for a check-in call from Seth—which gave him the chance to tell his brother about Simone and her indirect link to their grandfather.

"I'll be damned. So we finally have a clue why the old man had that property in Maine," Seth mused. "A mistress. I guess that's not really a surprise, given Gramps's history with women. But that's still a helluva house to set up a little side fling. There has to be more to it."

"Maybe. Simone's looking around now. Did you run across any stored suitcases, boxes, anything like that?"

"Not me. Actually, now that I think about it, Zach might have said something about some stuff in the attic. To tell you the truth, I think he forgot about them."

"Now there's a coincidence," Michael said wryly. "When you were here, seems I remember you mentioning there were a few choice antiques, well worth selling if not keeping. I notice they're still here. Seems you both suffered the exact same kind of memory lapse. Downright amazing, wouldn't you say?"

"Hey. My mind *may* have been on Samantha—"

"May? *May?* Zach hasn't talked about anything but Kirstin since Christmas. You're even more hopeless about Sam."

Seth, being Seth, couldn't take a ribbing without getting in the last word. "I can hear you laughing—but you'd better watch yourself in that house. We both told you, didn't we? The magic in that place is catching."

How the mighty do fall, Michael thought dryly as he hung up the phone. Zach had teased him about that mystical nonsense, too, but his youngest brother was a musician, creative to the point of damn near brilliance, but hardly famous for being levelheaded. Seth was a carpenter. He'd always been steady, practical and imminently logical—until he'd met Samantha. For him to tease about some 'magical power' in the house was the stuff of real humor. Love obviously had a sabotaging effect on his common sense.

Michael wasn't likely to suffer that problem. Not after Carla. Not ever again. Yet as he hooked up the computer, then the modem, he found his attention wandering, drifting to Simone.

"Lar, she's beautiful, isn't she? Soft-spoken. A real lady."

He lifted his head. For one curious instant, he thought he'd heard someone speaking, but of course, there was no one there. He picked up a braided tangle of electric cords and glared at it balefully.

"I saw the way ye looked at her, lad. Ye looked keelhauled, ye did, and I surely commiserate. Lar, that mouth was as tempting as a rosebud. And those eyes."

With a frown, Michael started fitting prongs into sockets. He wasn't *really* hearing a man's low-pitched baritone; it was more an involuntary whisper coming from his own mind. Weird. Even a little eerie, but to a point logical and understandable. He hadn't slept well in a blue moon; he was so tired he couldn't see straight, and hell, this exasperating hookup project was enough to temporarily unhinge any man. Besides, she was in the house. Knowing she was around, he was naturally going to think about her.

She hadn't been what he expected. That was the sole reason for the charge of hormones prowling through his bloodstream. His guess about Paula Stanford had been way off the mark— Who would have dreamed that efficient-sounding voice would belong to a female barracuda? But Simone... He'd been so sure, so positive, that she'd be shy and plain. Not a woman who would affect him. Not a woman who would make him feel...keelhauled.

They shared a pair of reprehensible relatives. Maybe that was part of it. He never anticipated finding anyone who was weighed down by the same kind of past. But that didn't precisely explain his bewildering reaction to her. It didn't explain—at all—why he was still thinking about her mouth, her eyes, the way her silvery-fine hair swished around her throat when she moved, that mischievous humor in her expression when she was holding back a smile.

"Ye ken imagine her naked, can't ye, lad? Between the sheets in the dark. She's got a fanny on her, thank the Lord. I canna abide skinny women meself. And ye ken imagine her wrapped around ye, all warm and soft, just for ye. Hot, just for you..."

Michael yanked off his glasses and pinched the bridge of his nose. Okay, for maybe three seconds, he'd imagined her in his bed. There was no excuse for such an adolescent fantasy. It was just that she wasn't as cool and poised as he first thought; he'd seen the vulnerability in her eyes and gotten the damn fool idea that she'd been hurt, and the next thing his mind flashed to was a picture of her in his bed; she was naked and beneath him and he was taking real, *real* good care of her.

How arrogant and stupid could a grown man get? He didn't know her. He had no reason to think she'd been hurt, no reason to think he'd ever be on a special wavelength with her. His failure with Carla had underlined how completely he misread women. The fantasy was a joke, a product of what abstinence and a too-long stretch of celibacy could do to a man's mind. It wasn't personal. It wasn't *her*.

"Michael..."

Yeah, he heard his name called. He ignored it. He wasn't suckering into that voice of temptation again. A winsome, salty breeze filtered through the open window. It ruffled the hair on his nape when he hunched over the computer to connect the keyboard.

"Michael?"

He whipped his head around. So he hadn't imagined her voice; Simone *was* there, standing in the doorway. But looking distinctly different than she had earlier. So different that he could feel the slow seep of a masculine grin before he could stop it. Holy spit. Her spotless white slacks now had dirt smudges; her knit top was hanging askew from one shoulder, and unless he was mistaken, her silky soft hair was decorated with cobwebs.

"You really have your hands full in here, don't you?" She gestured to all the computer debris with a guilty look. "I'm sorry to interrupt, but I'm afraid I have a little problem."

"Yeah?" Even dirty and disheveled, she reminded him of peppermint ice cream. Pink and white. Cool, sweet, yet with enough spice to bite into. The image lodged in his mind with the tenacity of a tick. Simone was a near stranger; she was nothing like ice cream, and his confounded response to the woman had to stop.

"I found my grandmother's things," she told him.

"Well, that's terrific."

"Not exactly." She sighed ruefully. "I'm afraid there isn't just a box of mementos. There are trunks. Huge trunks. About ten of them. Diaries, books, all kinds of things. Michael, I'm not sure what to do, but I have to say— It's going to take me an age to go through it all."

Michael strode forward in a flash. A nice, tangible problem. *That,* he knew how to handle. "How about if you just show me? These trunks are in the attic, right?"

"You already knew about them?"

"I just got off the phone with my brother. He mentioned some things in the attic, but I haven't been up there. Don't even know where it is."

She led the way. Up the split staircase, down the dark hall, then up more steps and through a round-framed door to a set of dusty wooden stairs.

It was dark up there. Closed-up musty. Heat shimmered from the naked beams and rough plank floor. Lacy webs of cobwebs draped the corners, as thick as curtains. Still, two round windows at both ends of the long room reflected enough light so he could see the steamer trunks she was talking about. They were huge.

"I couldn't open a couple of them. They're locked. Actually I think they were all locked, but the latches were so rusty that most of them gave pretty easily. It's just that they're absolutely loaded with *stuff*, Michael. I never anticipated anything like this."

Neither had he. Hunkering down, he pushed up one lid to take a look—and abruptly blinked. The trunk was crammed with all sorts of debris, but the top layer was some kind of embarrassing women's underwear. Corsets and wires and ribbons were piled helter-skelter. Gingerly he held up a faded red satin robe with torn black lace. "Well," he said dryly, "for absolutely positive this sure couldn't be my grandfather's."

"I just wish it weren't my grandmother's," Simone muttered. "It looks like something a hooker would wear in a bordello."

"Maybe it's just what women wore sixty years ago?"

"Trust me. Not *nice* women." Her cheeks flushed. "Anyway, there's more here than unmentionables." From another trunk, she lifted out a light prism and seaman's eyescope to show him. "There's just all *kinds* of things. Including diaries—about a half-dozen of

them, each covering a year's span of time. My grandmother told me those were here. In fact, she told me
they were mine, that she specifically wanted me to read
them . . . but I feel uneasy about it. It feels like prying.
And I wouldn't just be prying into her private business, but your grandfather's, too."

"If you're asking my permission, it's not a sweat.
Like I told you, nothing you could find about my
grandfather could possibly surprise me." He cuffed the
back of his neck with a rough palm. "But damned if I
know how to handle this. It'd take some heavyweight
man power to move even one of these trunks downstairs."

"I know. I already figured out it'd be easier to sort
it all out right here, then handle the trunks when they
were empty. But I'm afraid it would take me days.
There's just so much. I'd be under your feet, in your
way."

She was obviously troubled at causing him a problem, and Michael responded instinctively. "Look— If
you're volunteering to handle this, you'd be doing me
a favor. I'd have to get rid of it all somehow, anyway."

"Still—"

The attic door suddenly blew shut below, startling
both of them. Temporarily the problem of the trunks
was forgotten.

"How . . . odd," Simone said uneasily. "It was breezy
this morning, but hardly enough to make a door slam.
The wind must have really picked up."

"Wind in the upstairs hall? Not likely." They both
headed down the stairs at the same time, Simone just
a breath ahead of him. She reached the door first, but
when she tried to turn the knob, it wouldn't budge.

"Michael . . . I think it's locked."

"Can't be. It takes a key to lock that kind of door, and there's no one in the house but us." When he reached out and tried it, though, the knob refused to turn. The door wasn't stuck. It was just plain locked. "This doesn't make sense," he said impatiently.

"Are we trapped up here?"

"No. Relax, all right? Everything's fine." He dug in his front pocket and produced a ring of dangling keys. "Afraid I have a real boring habit of always being prepared."

"You call that boring? I'd call it an outstanding relief. For a second there, I had visions of starving in a garret like in some Victorian melodrama. I mean, who knows how long it would be before anyone found us?" But she relaxed, the instant she saw the keys. He got another one of those smiles again. The sensuous dip of a grin, the crinkle of mischief around her eyes. "You think there was a ghost trying to lock us in?"

"You believe in ghosts?"

"Heavens, no."

Neither did Michael, yet for a curious moment, time seemed to suspend. He'd isolated the marked attic key, had it in his hand, ready to aim for the lock in the door. It was just... He hadn't realized how close she was. The attic steps were narrow; the well at the bottom so cramped that there was barely room for both of them to stand.

Unwilling, unwanted, his mind framed a picture of her in that red satin robe. There were no *ghosts* in that damned attic, no ludicrous haunting echoes of their past relatives. The boundaries of right and wrong and morality had always been cut-and-dried to Michael. But if her grandmother looked anything like Simone,

Michael suddenly understood how his grandfather had succumbed to temptation.

She'd started out that morning so neat and tailored, with an I-can-handle-anything poise and confidence. Now he wondered if her choice of clothes was just a mask, a protection she wore against the world. She didn't seem aware that her foray in the attic had made her look all...undone. Her hair was softly tumbled and disheveled. Her skin was warm, damp at the throat and brow, that skin heat giving off the scent of some vaguely flowery perfume. Camelias, he thought. Something fragile, sweet, delicate. And it was emotion that made her eyes look so brilliant. He could too easily imagine the warmth and vulnerability in her eyes if she were looking at a lover. Imagine one of those smiles that stir-fried his libido, directed just at him, just for him. She so obviously wasn't the red-satin-robe type. Not in public. But with a lover she could be honest with, a lover she wanted to please, Michael wondered what she'd wear, what she'd be like, if she really felt the freedom to turn off that Poise and Control button and just let go.

Her smile faded over a heart's breath. Her eyes shot to his, and clung. She was as aware of him as he was of her, because the breath caught in her throat in that spin of a second.

He wasn't going to kiss her. He was positive of that. He barely knew her and his failure with Carla was as fresh as a bullet wound. He wasn't going near any woman. There was simply no chance of his kissing her.

Yet the impulse was almost irresistible. She moved. Or he did. Maybe she swayed toward him? So close he could see her parted lips and the pulse beating, beating, in the soft hollow of her throat. It hadn't occurred to him that she found him attractive, that she'd noticed him as a man the way he'd indelibly noticed she was a woman. It seemed she had. Her eyes had the shimmer and shine of emotion, both vulnerability and unsureness, but also something softer. Desire. She looked straight at him as if she couldn't break away, as if a spell of magic was holding her still. She wasn't even breathing. Wasn't even trying.

A muted grumbling sound broke the spell. She blinked. So did he. Color shot to her pale cheeks as she clapped a hand over her abdomen.

"Ah... Ms. Hartman... was that your stomach growling?"

"Heavens, no. My stomach would never be so rude as to growl in public." She swallowed, quickly, on a rueful chuckle. "I just remembered that I skipped breakfast, though."

"So'd I. In fact, this whole day has gone so far astray from the blueprint I'd planned that I'm not sure what happened—but it's about time we both called it quits and broke for lunch."

"Agreed," she said with a smile.

He lifted the key and efficiently plugged it into the lock. It only took a second to push open the door and step out in the nice, cool, drafty hall. Safe, he thought. That bewilderingly strange moment was over. God knew what had happened there—or almost happened—but for damn sure, he'd be careful it didn't happen again.

Simone meant to drive back to her bed and breakfast in Bar Harbor. Michael had brought up lunch, but that never meant he intended an invitation for her to

share the meal with him. Actually she was pretty sure
he didn't. It was just that he aimed for the kitchen
when they both headed downstairs. And she followed
him there, only because they were still talking about
how to resolve the problem of the trunks.

Before he knew it, he'd slapped together enough
sandwiches for both of them.

Before she knew it, they seemed to be walking out to
the beach with a picnic sack and a blanket. In princi-
ple, sharing the makeshift lunch was fine by her. She
would have had to shower and change clothes before
finding a place to eat in town. Still, she'd been comfortable with Michael until that strange moment in the
attic.

Now she felt unsettled. There'd been no kiss, no
pass, but Simone was uneasily aware that there might
have been. She'd never been so drawn to a stranger.
She'd almost forgotten what it felt like, to have a man
arouse that edgy, electric, hopeful feeling. That hunger to connect with someone who mattered. That
woman's need to reach out to a man who moved her.

Drat. With her history with men, she should know
better. Freud had a lot to say about the dangers of repression, but Freud was a guy. Simone was doing just
fine repressed. She just had to remember to *stay* good
and solidly repressed around Michael.

He spread the blanket on a square flat stone, high
above the water, as she looked around. This was no
tame Florida beach. Huge boulders dominated the
shoreline, backdropped by tall stands of virgin spruce
and white pines. A round white lighthouse sat on a
jagged peninsula of land, clearly part of Michael's
property. Further down, past a saucer-shaped cove,
rooftops caught the sun—vacationers' cottages—and

on the water, colorful sails dipped and zigzagged, playing tag with the breeze. It wasn't hot. Not with that tufty, summer ocean breeze, but the sun beat down with sleepy, somnolent warmth.

Their perch of rock was secluded, private, and she started to relax.

Michael held up two sandwiches. "You want roast beef or roast beef? Take your time making a decision."

In spite of her staunch determination to stay repressed, she couldn't quite hold back a grin. "I think...roast beef."

"First hurdle down. Unfortunately we're still a long way from home free. I don't suppose there's a prayer you like horseradish?"

"Love it."

He raised one suspicious brow. "I don't want to know if you're just being tactful. I slathered it on the sandwiches before I had the brains to ask you, so I'm afraid you're stuck."

"No, really. I like it."

"Yeah? Well, now comes the next test. Dark beer. And damn, I forgot glasses." He lifted his head from the sack and saw the expression on her face. "Aw, hell. You're a teetotaler?"

"No. I've just never had dark beer. It's not a problem. I'm more than willing to give it a try."

"It's okay if you don't like it. I'm just short on extra groceries until I have a chance to make a serious store run, but we could easily bring a pitcher of ice water from the house." He cocked a leg, leaning back against a grainy stretch of rock with a sandwich in his hand. "Let's settle this trunk business, okay? How long are you going to be in Maine?"

"Four weeks."

"You planned on needing four weeks to look for your grandmother's stuff?"

She shook her head and swallowed a mouthful. "I manage a ski shop in Colorado. Steamboat Springs. Summer's a slow time. My family's always headed for the ocean on summer vacations, so I know this area around Bar Harbor. Since I was stuck coming for my grandmother, I cleared the decks so I could hopefully combine a vacation at the same time."

"You're originally from Colorado, then? I'll be damned. So was my whole family—including my grandfather. At least we have a clue how our infamous lovers managed to meet each other, if they were both from the same neck of the country. And your Julia was fond of this area in Maine?"

Simone nodded and took her first sip of dark ale from the long-necked bottle. The taste was heavy, pungent, but it washed down the morning's thirst wonderfully.

Michael watched her expression, checking to see if she found the drink palatable, and then reached for another sandwich. "Anyway. So you have some time. How about if I set you up in one of the rooms upstairs, and you just come over when it works out for you?" He thought. "I could hire the man power to cart the trunks over to your place, but I don't see what that would accomplish. What do you have, a rented room? Not enough space there. The attic would probably be too dark and dusty to work in, but there's a half-dozen spare bedrooms. I want to show the house—I need that white elephant sold—but that isn't going to happen overnight, and one messy room isn't going to make any difference."

"Sounds fine. If you're sure I won't be in your way. You're really being great about this."

"Seems to me it's a shared problem. I'd be stuck with handling all that stuff if you didn't want it." He hesitated, then said quietly, "I have the feeling that it matters a lot to you. Finding those things of your grandmother's."

"It does," she admitted. "My grandmother was really strange about the whole thing. She doesn't even want to see the things herself—she just didn't want them falling in the hands of strangers. But other members of the family could have come. She wanted me. She was really insistent about my having them. She seemed very sure they would mean something personal to me."

"And you think that's true?"

"I don't know. I'd like some answers, I know that."

"What kind of answers?"

Simone drew up her knees and wrapped her arms around them. If Michael were anyone else, she would have deflected the question and steered the conversation to something easier. But if she went through those diaries, some of her family's secrets—and his—were bound to come out in the wash. There was just no purpose in hiding them. Still she hesitated. "Am I going to bore you to death if I give you a quick Hartman history?"

"I promise. No."

That slow smile of his, she thought, was dangerous to her mental health. Maybe he looked at all women with that same kind of interest and intensity, but it made her feel buttery and vulnerable and hopelessly female. Talking about Julia, thankfully, was guaranteed to put her back on the Repression Track right quickly. "I don't know why my grandmother stayed married, when she was obviously unhappy with my grandfather. But she did, and way later in life, they eventually had one child. My mother. Mom grew up knowing that *her* mom played around. And when she grew up—just like Julia—she couldn't stay away from the good-looking charmers. My dad was a drinker and a gambler. She divorced him and married his clone— another handsome rogue who couldn't hold a job worth spit. Am I boring you yet?"

"No."

Simone lifted her face to study his expression, but he truthfully didn't seem to be going to sleep yet. So she kept on. "My mom had three daughters—first me, then Laura and Rolly. Laura's already been divorced. She's only twenty-three. Rolly's living with a guy who's taking her for every dime." She shrugged. "Half the world comes from a dysfunctional family. Ours isn't particularly special. But having bad judgment about men is a real pattern with the Hartman women—and it all started with Julia." She gestured vaguely, trying to find the right words. "I'd just like to know more about her. What made her so...wild, so selfish and irresponsible. Because what she did had some long-reaching effects on the rest of us. Can you under-stand?"

"More than you know," Michael said quietly. "Hell. I swear it's eerie. Everything you said about your fam-ily has an echo in mine. The same roots. The same pattern with the opposite sex."

"Really?" A gull screamed in the shallows. The breeze brushed a strand of hair on her cheek, and she pushed it away, unaware of anything but the magnetic pull in his eyes. He really did seem to understand.

"You didn't say...and maybe it's prying to ask...if you've had the same bad luck as the other women in your family."

"Oh, yeah." A seep of a sigh escaped her. Maybe it was a sigh of relief. He'd given her an opening to put her cards on the table, and it struck her as terrifically wise to take it. "Some people are good at relationships. Definitely not me," she said firmly.

"Me, either."

"I like men fine. My partner in the store is a man. I have lots of men friends. But no way, no how, am I interested in becoming involved with anyone in a serious way right now."

"I like women fine. But I'm not looking for any kind of serious involvement, either."

"It's been my own fault. Those relationships that haven't worked out. I'm not blaming anyone else. But I'll be damned if I'm going to turn out like my grandmother, with a track record of bad judgment and hurting people—"

"I just failed at a ten-year marriage. My fault, nothing to do with my grandfather, except that he had a helluva history of hurting women and probably couldn't define commitment with a dictionary. One of the reasons the divorce still stings is that, my whole life, I swore I'd never turn out anything like him."

"—Even if I were unusually attacted to someone—"

"—Even if I were really interested in someone for the first time in a blue moon—"

"I—" Simone abruptly stopped talking. It finally filtered through her brain, that he'd been echoing every sentiment she'd said. Michael seemed to realize it before she did. He looked momentarily baffled, as confused as if someone had pitched him a curveball out of nowhere . . . and then his mouth slowly tipped in a dry masculine grin.

"If you want to know the truth—I can't remember being on a wavelength with a woman, Hartman."

"I can't remember being on an honest wavelength with a man, Connor."

"I hate to suggest something so outlandish or crazy, but do you think there's an insane chance we might actually be . . . friends?"

She chuckled at his droll tone. He made it sound like the idea of being *friends* was mystifying, revolutionary. A feeling of warmth unfurled inside her like a fragile petal opening for the sunlight. She couldn't remember feeling safe with a man. Safe from risk, safe from hurt, comfortable expressing herself because he felt the same way. She'd never felt that kind of bond with anyone.

It lasted for all of seven minutes.

She picked up their lunch debris, and folded it all into the sack. Michael shook out the blanket and rolled it under an arm. Lunch was over. They were a little strange with each other— How could they not be, after expressing some uncomfortable-to-admit feelings like that? But from the quiet warmth in Michael's eyes, she guessed he was relieved and reassured that those things had been said. They were going to be spending some time together, but that didn't have to be tricky just because she was a woman and he was a man. Not now that they both knew where they stood. The rules were clear. They both liked the boundaries. They both . . . agreed.

Feeling lighthearted, absolutely flooded with a rare sensation of well-being, Simone started climbing down the rough boulders to head for the yard. Ocean spray made the gray stones shine like silver. Her sandal slipped and the heel caught in a crevice.

She tipped. Tried to right herself. Overbalanced.

And toppled straight back into Michael.

Four

Her ankle scraped against a rock as she collided into Michael. He let out a startled *"Ooomph."* The picnic sack flew out of her hands; the blanket flew out of his.

Instinctively he tried to grab her, to break her fall, but it didn't save either of them a tumble. She landed with an elbow in his ribs. He crashed straight on the boulders. It happened so fast. It took a second before she caught her breath, another second before her mind registered mortification at being such a clumsy klutz... and another, when she abruptly realized how intimately—and embarrassingly—she was lying between his thighs.

"Lord, I'm sorry. I couldn't help it. The rock was slippery, and my sandal just shot out from under me. Are you okay? I..." She twisted, her hands groping for purchase so she could lift her weight off him. When her palm connected with his muscled thigh, though, she was embarrassed again and instantly let go. She fell back a second time, her knee tangling with his and her elbow re-stabbing his ribs. She heard a strange rumbling sound and lifted her head.

Blinding sunlight hit her straight in the eyes, but she could still see the rise and fall of his chest. He wasn't just chuckling: he was outright laughing. "Ever consider licensing your knees and elbows as lethal weapons? I *know* you're trying to get up, but I swear I'm gonna need an ambulance if you don't quit helping. And are you all right?"

"Beyond dying of embarrassment, you mean?"

"Hey, don't waste feeling embarrassed on my account. This was a rare treat. I've never had a woman throw herself into my arms before. For sure, never with that kind of passionate enthusiasm."

"Oh, God. Really I wasn't—"

"Simone. I know. I was just teasing." Laughter still flashed in his eyes as he scooted back. His hands clamped on her shoulders, anchoring her steady so that she couldn't fall again—and probably saving himself another elbow in the ribs. Once he managed to stand up, he hooked her wrists and pull her up next to him. "Let's check for damage control, okay? That was quite a tumble. You sure you're not bruised or hurt?"

Her ankle stung. She'd lost a sandal. Her right hip throbbed like fire. "I'm fine," she said, which wasn't at all true. The minor injuries didn't bother her and she didn't care about the sandal. Her lungs just seemed temporarily engorged on oxygen. Any second now, she was going to remember that handy little trick about exhaling. Since he was chuckling, she wanted to chuckle, too. Everyone was a klutz sometimes. It wasn't really that mortifying. But the feeling of his hands running down her arms had a manic effect on her heartbeat. Those moments when she'd been clapped between his thighs were still affecting her blood pressure. His gaze on her face was creating another problem. He wasn't looking her over in any sexual way, more just scanning her features to make sure she was really okay. But he'd never be checking a man over. Not like that. His eyes were gentle, caring, reflecting—whether or not he knew it—that he was the kind of man who automatically took care of a woman.

"I'm not sure those pants are ever gonna be white again, but you seem okay. And it could have been worse, right? We could have both ended up pitching off the rocks into the water, and then had a real mess. Hell, is that blood on your ankle?"

"No."

"Sure it is. Damn—"

She wasn't sure if he said "damn" because of discovering the rouged scrape on her ankle, or because he suddenly looked up, and caught her eyes on him. All she knew was that he seemed to freeze for that instant.

Salt spray splashed below. The dancing breeze caught a ribbon strand of her hair and plastered it against her forehead. Slowly he raised his hand to brush it away. "Simone." His voice was suddenly thick and low. Whether he was calling her or scolding her, she had no idea. He swore again, in that same husky male rasp, and then startling her—maybe startling him, too—his arms wrapped around her.

Maybe she'd been asking for a kiss. The burr of guilt prickled her conscience, realizing that he must have read some kind of invitation in her face—even if she hadn't meant it, even if she knew better.

But her pulse skidded down a long, slippery hill when his lips touched hers. His mouth was warm and mobile. He tasted of the same spice as that rich, dark ale. If he were just aggressive, she'd have known what to do. But Michael . . . He kissed her as if he'd been on a hundred-year fast, and was just discovering hunger in the form of her taste, her scent, her touch. It wasn't as though he planned that first kiss to ignite a warehouse of dynamite.

But Lord, neither had she. That first slow kiss seeped into another, then another. Nobody—nobody—had ever kissed her with that kind of total immersion, as if his whole universe centered on her, as if the sky could have fallen and he wouldn't have noticed or cared. Their noses bumped. It didn't make him smile. It didn't make him stop. His hands swept down her back as he slanted his head, taking her mouth again, then taking her tongue. His first kisses had been deep. This one dived straight for intimate treasure.

There was no romance left in her soul. She knew that for sure. She'd stamped out that nasty weed, toughened up, turned into a practical realist who, thank God, was absolutely nothing like the other women in her family. She wasn't prey to fantasies or fairy tales. She wasn't prey to dreams.

His whiskers scraped her cheek. Her pulse fluttered like a sail in a gale wind. She had the impossible feeling that her sturdy world was tipping, and the only thing she could hold on to was him. She'd heard him say that he'd been married, heard him say that he was divorced, yet there was no expertise in his kisses, no practiced skill in his touch. Heat. It poured off his long lean body. He kissed her with the urgency of need, the

tenderness of wonder, as if he'd just found something
irresistibly precious and damned if he could let her go.

She wasn't precious. She wasn't crazy. But he made
her mouth ache and her blood rush with yearnings
she'd thought were long buried. When his hands slid
down to her bottom, cupping her closer, cupping her
to him, her breasts tightened in automatic, instinctive
response.

She was no spring-fed virgin. She knew what passion was, but not what it felt like to... connect. With
a man so tuned to her mind and body that he might
have been her lover for a thousand years.

The sun burned behind her closed eyes when his lips
trailed to her neck. His hands rubbed, stroked,
claimed. She could feel his heartbeat against her chest,
becoming staccato and urgent, making her shiver from
deep inside. He was aroused. She'd have to be nuts not
to recognize the earthy, hot pressure against her abdomen; his whole body was tightening, tensing, hard-
ening.

Fear whispered through her nerves. Not a fear that
he would hurt her, but something else, an instinct, pri-
mal and pure female, that this was a man who could
take her under. She'd never tangled with fire. She'd
never aroused the deep, dark side of a man's passion,
but she had the heady, delicious, shaky sensation that
she could with Michael.

His palm swept from her hips to her ribs, then
molded over the small tight mound of one breast. Her
breath caught like a trapped web. He hadn't touched
her bare flesh; she was still wearing a knit top and bra,
yet his touch made her feel as vulnerable as if she already belonged to him. His palm, his fingertips, moved
up, to the hollow in her throat, the exposed fragile line

of her collarbone, to the edge of her jaw. He opened his eyes.

And stopped.

She didn't know why. The look in his eyes could have melted icebergs; that desire was for her, as intense as a blaze and as intimate as a burn. Yet he jerked back from her abruptly. From the expression in his eyes, he couldn't have been more bewildered or shocked if a sniper had just jabbed an uzi in his back.

"Simone..." He swallowed hard, but his voice was still hoarse and raw. "I'm damned if I know how that happened, but I'm sorry. Real sorry."

"It's all right." She told herself it wasn't a lie. Any moment now, that silly, silly feeling of belonging to him would disappear. Any moment now, her limbs were going to stop feeling logy and liquid. Any moment now, she was going to stop feeling like she'd had an experience of the third kind, encountered something rare and special that she'd never even known existed.

"No, it's not all right. You have every right to be angry with me."

"No, I... no." She wasn't angry. She didn't know what she was. Confused, embarrassed, unsure. Michael was transforming in front her eyes, the incredibly compelling lover gone and the businessman Michael taking his place, a man in control, a man who valued logical and rational behavior. She told herself she was relieved. Enormously relieved.

"It was... an accident. It won't happen again, I swear. And it was just a few kisses, nothing more. Nothing *happened*."

She bobbed her head in violent agreement.

"I wasn't expecting ... how much we'd have in common, how easy it would be to talk with you. I don't feel that kind of empathy with many people, and never a woman, never that fast and ... aw, hell, am I putting my foot in my mouth by admitting being attracted to you?"

She shook her head with equal violence. It was okay that he was attracted to her. It was okay that she was attracted to him. Getting it out in the open was like defusing a bomb with words. Hormones. Chemistry. Attraction. No big deal. And his voice, now, was gathering steam. It was working for him, too. "I don't want you to think anything's changed. We have a head start on being honest with each other, don't we? You don't want to be involved. Neither do I. Being honest about a problem is the best way I know to put a lid on it. If we're going to spend some time together, I don't want you uncomfortable around me, afraid I'm going to come on to you—"

"I'm not worried."

His knuckles brushed her chin, tilting her face. His eyes searched hers. "You sure?"

Worry chewed on her nerves, a vague edginess that Simone had been trying to shake for two days now. She knew the cause. It just wasn't that easy to make the problem disappear.

As she carted the box of diaries downstairs from the attic, she heard a telephone ring below. It only rang once— Michael answered it from the library. Later that afternoon, the real estate agent was scheduled to bring some people to see the house, but right now, Simone had no doubt that his computer was on, his fax was screaming and his whole army of electronic equipment was battling business.

He worked too hard, she mused. Although she'd been staying at the bed and breakfast, she'd spent hours with him now, long enough to know that he had twin sons he adored, that he was close with his brothers, that his ex-wife was named Carla and the failure of his marriage really preyed on his mind.

Simone had mentally pictured Carla as a witless goose. It wasn't a hard conclusion to reach. Michael was one rare kahuna, an old-fashioned guy with values like integrity and honor and honesty. The wrapping on the package was a sneaky sense of humor and a dizzying amount of sex appeal. A woman with a brain didn't walk out on a man like that. Personally, Simone would have handcuffed him to a bedpost where no other woman could conceivably get a look at him....

That restless edginess chewed on her nerves again. She'd sworn—violently sworn—to keep her mind off Michael.

Blowing a strand of hair from her cheeks, she dropped the box and heeled off her sneakers. Usually she worked in the attic. She really didn't want to carry things up and down, tracking dust and cobwebs through his house, but Michael had offered the use of this blue bedroom. She was grateful for the choice. A storm was forecast, gray popcorn-shaped clouds already clustering over the Atlantic, and the heat had been unlivably stifling under the attic eaves.

She curled up on the cushioned window seat and glanced around the room. A gusty breeze made the white lace curtains tuft and sink, the fresh air cooling her damp cheeks. The bedroom was clearly meant for

spare guests, small, and not much furniture beyond a
bed, table and chest. But the room had character and
charm—a slanted ceiling, one wall paneled for inset
bookcases, and the window seat view of the lighthouse and rocky shore. Curiously she noted the
threadwork of scars and cracks on one pale blue wall.
The house was three hundred years old, so it was hardly
surprising the wall had cracks, but it actually looked as
if someone had taken a hammer to that spot and plastered the flaw.

*What difference does it make? Quit dithering and get
to work, Hartman.*

Impatiently she pulled the box of diaries onto her
lap. It had taken hours to isolate and separate her
grandmother's records from the wealth of debris in the
trunks. She wanted to go through them. If there were
clues to all those belongings upstairs, her logical best
chance of finding them was by reading the diaries. And
it wasn't like she was prying into her grandmother's
private life. Julia had not only given her permission;
she'd been pigheaded stubborn about Simone being the
only one in the family to touch these things.

Only her feelings about the entire project had
changed as of two days ago. Michael was the difference. She'd tried, but she couldn't get that embrace out
of her mind. Fires were caused by faulty wiring, only
Simone had never discovered an electrical short in her
system before. She'd come apart in his arms. She'd
come alive, wantonly, shamelessly, embarrassingly
alive. He could have taken her on that rock, and she
wouldn't have said anything more than "please." It
worried and scared her, that she'd behaved so totally
out of character.

And it was still worrying her. With a frown grooved in her forehead, she drew up her knees and lifted the first leather-bound diary in her lap. Chronologically it was the first, dated 1929. Her fingertip traced the ragged, worn cover.

She wasn't *afraid* of opening it. At least, not exactly. There was no prayer she could possibly discover that she was anything like her grandmother. She was a realist. Not a romantic. Responsible, not wild. She had morals and principles, and dammit, as much as she loved her feisty and irascible grandmother, Julia couldn't define a moral worth spit. In the vernacular of her day, she'd been a tramp. She'd let hormones rule her life, always falling for men she couldn't have and, yeah— Simone knew exactly what that was like.

She hadn't forgotten John, or Bryan. One mistake in judgment was understandable, but discovering Bryan was married had been a crusher. She'd split from both relationships faster than a speeding bullet, damnably aware that she could too easily fall into the bad-luck-with-men pattern that plagued all the Hartman women. It wasn't going to happen to her. Unlike Julia, she learned from past mistakes. She'd gotten tough. She'd gotten smart. She'd become a cynic about romance, and a realist about herself and men.

That armor had proved wonderfully invincible— She'd long stopped worrying that she was anything like her grandmother. Until Michael. Her response to him had been bewildering, crazy, disturbing. Like the nagging buzz of a mosquito, she just couldn't seem to get it off her mind. Determinedly she opened the leather diary, thumbed to the first page and forced herself to concentrate. How absolutely silly, to think reading these diaries was any threat to her. Sillier yet, to dwell on one flukish moment in time that would never happen again. Michael had obviously forgotten the embrace. He wasn't reserved around her; if anything, they talked with the rare ease of old friends. They'd laughed a dozen times. They were simply…cronies…until this problem of her grandmother's belongings was resolved.

The sooner she got to it, the sooner she would be out of his hair and out of his life.

She focused her attention on the faded feminine script, penned so carefully in black ink. The first lines leaped out at her.

October 29, 1929. The market crashed today. They're calling it Black Thursday. I haven't left my room, haven't talked to anyone. There's no purpose. There is no way I can get out of the marriage now.

Simone didn't know how much time passed. An hour? Maybe two? The telephone rang several times. She was almost sure she heard a car door slam, and her mind registered that the people were here to look at the house. None of the extraneous noises affected her concentration.

It was only when she finished the first diary that she even looked up. Charcoal clouds had completely blocked the sun. The pale blue bedroom had a dusty stillness, a ghostly quiet. There was no one in the room with her, but it felt that way, as if a young nineteen-year-old Julia was right there, close enough to touch her.

Quickly she uncoiled from the window seat, grabbed the diary and headed for the stairs. What she'd learned about Julia had been unexpected, but what she'd learned about Benjamin was even more so. Knowing Michael's complex feelings about his grandfather, she was sure he'd appreciate knowing what she'd discovered.

Michael saw her legs first—the smooth, bare calves as they bounded down the stairs. She was wearing a denim skirt with a peppermint-stick striped blouse, her blond hair pulled neatly back with a simple pink ribbon. The attire, he'd come to know, was typically Simone. Neat, modest, tailored. Nothing to explain why one look at her made his heartbeat suddenly trip and stumble.

Halfway down the split stairs, she peered over the banister. Her eyes widened when she saw the crowd of people in the hall, and she abruptly spun around.

"Simone." It was an impulse, clipping up the half-dozen steps to catch up with her. The impulse was practical—even logical—and had absolutely nothing to do with that strange thrum in his pulse.

She turned when he called her name, and motioned to the small leather book she was carrying. "I just wanted to tell you something. It'll wait," she said swiftly.

"If you could spare a few minutes, you could save me from a fate worse than death," he murmured under his breath.

"Ah, I see. . . . Ms. Sharkess. She giving you a hard time again?" she murmured under hers. He caught the dance of humor in her eyes. He caught her smile.

She seemed to have totally recovered from his abominable behavior on the beach days before. He hadn't, but now wasn't the moment to dwell on that problem.

He had a houseful of people, and with an ounce of luck, a potential sale going down. Paula Stanford *was* giving him a hard time—the confounded woman looked like a hooker in a tight-fitting chartreuse suit, and she made him *damned* uneasy whenever she looked at him—but he sure couldn't fault her for doing her job. Her judgment in picking good prey couldn't be faulted.

The potential buyers she'd brought were a Japanese family. Mr. Suisami was a physicist who worked in a private lab in D.C. Judging from his new BMW and the cut of his suit, Michael wasn't worried that the man could afford a vacation retreat in Maine. His wife was a small-boned woman, shy, quiet, with three children, and from her plump rounded abdomen, Michael suspected there was another bun in the oven. His sons would have been climbing the walls by now, exploring the whole house at the speed of light. Not hers. Their faces were all solemn, and they trailed behind their mother as if they were peas in a pod.

Michael had made more money in stocks than land, but it didn't take a real estate magnate to know that it was the woman who made or broke the sale of any house. Paula had latched herself onto Mr. Suisami. That left him with the mom and her brood of ducklings. The problem was the language barrier. Mrs. Suisami appeared to know only one word in English. Nice.

He'd shown her the sun room with the jalousie windows and view of the beach and woods. She'd bobbed her head and said, "Nice." He'd shown her the library, assured her all his computer equipment would be gone, and pointed out the ample space for books and furniture. She'd bobbed her head and said, "Nice." He'd shown her the kitchen, with the freshly varnished oak cabinets and the huge back-room pantry. She'd bobbed her head and said, "Nice."

"I don't think she understands a word I say," Michael muttered to Simone. "All she does is smile at me. I have no idea if I'm getting through."

"And you think I could be of help? Michael, I don't speak Japanese."

"You speak *woman,* don't you? I mean, you know what a woman would want to know about a house. Just stick with me when I take her upstairs to see the bedrooms, okay?"

Before she had the chance to argue with him, Paula called out, "Michael?" Hell, the chartreuse bat was headed his way again. Simone shot him a look when he grabbed her hand, but she didn't really seem to mind being dragged downstairs for introductions. Paula's "Hi again!" was breezy; Mr. Suisami pumped her hand with a polite bow, and Mrs. Suisami and her entire brood nodded their heads in greeting. "Nice," Mrs. Suisami said. Michael looked at Simone meaningfully. *See? What'd I tell you?*

He guessed it would go better with her around, and it did. By the time the clan clattered upstairs to check out the bedrooms, the youngest Suisami—a silent boy named Harry—was attached to her hand. Simone didn't have to know the house. She was warm and natural with the other woman, and she'd sized up each kid in seconds, had them chattering about which bedroom they'd pick to sleep in if they lived here. The only weird moment came when she pushed open the door to the master bedroom.

She did a double take, and then her gaze cut straight to his over the bob of heads. Michael washed a hand over his face. Hell, he forgot that she hadn't seen that particular room before. "Tell Mrs. Suisami that I didn't decorate it, okay? I had nothing to do with it."

But shy Mrs. Suisami had already stepped inside, and was saying, "Nice. *Nice!*" in a distinctly rapt tone of voice.

Simone's lips twitched. So did his, then. Possibly Mrs. Suisami wasn't so demure with her husband when the lights went out; the blatantly sexual decor certainly didn't seem to bother her. The flush on Simone's cheeks was far more telling.

"I don't believe this," she murmured dryly.

"The first time I saw it, neither did I."

"Good grief. It's like... an old-fashioned bachelor pit. A seduction lair. A set from a Valentino movie."

"You should try sleeping in it." Her eyes bounced to his again. He cleared his throat. "I meant—figuratively."

"It's okay. I never thought you meant anything funny. It's just a little embarrassing, isn't it? Thinking about our grandparents sleeping here."

"Exactly," he said. Little Harry tugged on her hand, saving him from having to say anything else.

It was true that he'd thought about his grandfather in this room, wondered and worried if Simone was going to find out that Benjamin had seduced her grandmother in that damn sultan's bed. But the last two nights, he'd awakened from troubling dreams in which Benjamin had no part. He had. *He'd* been doing the ruthless seducing. Both nights Simone had been wearing a simple pink-and-white nightshirt, her legs bare and her cheeks scrubbed—but all that wholesomeness had disappeared when he'd turned off the lamp. She'd transformed for him, as she'd transformed when he kissed her on the beach, into a sensual and wildly uninhibited lover.

In the dreams he'd created a romantic setting, champagne by moonlight, music, candles. She'd been wild for him, vulnerable, her heart laid raw and bare in passion. And he—of course—had been the best lover she'd ever had, the only man who understood her, the only man strong enough to meet her needs.

"Nice." Mrs. Suisami turned toward him with a sweet smile. "*Nice.*"

"Yeah," Michael said, "Real nice." He heard the ironic twist in his own voice, and pulled himself up short. A *nice* guy would put a fantasy like that in a mental wastebasket. His understanding of women was a matter of public record in divorce court. He didn't have a clue what any woman wanted or needed, much less Simone, and God knew where that romantic nonsense had come from. She'd laugh if a man tried to pull off anything like that. She was an imminently practical realist, had said so a half-dozen times.

So was he. But if he didn't understand women, he certainly understood business. Although he never expected the first fish to take the bait, the Suisami family was clearly crazy about the house. Herding the troops downstairs, he found Paula and Mr. Suisami in the parlor, talking money.

Paula had an avaricious gleam in her eyes. She could smell a sale as well as he could. Husband and wife conferred by themselves for several minutes; whatever Mrs. Suisami told him made Mr. Suisami reach inside his suit for his checkbook. Relief filled Michael. They were getting the house at a steal price. Normally it went against Michael's grain to get taken, but not this time. He wanted the house out of his hair, done, sold, the whole problem gone. It would still take a dog's age to close the deal, but earnest money was going down on the line.

Simone caught his eye. She winked with a subtle thumbs-up. He chuckled and started to move toward her. An odd clanking sound seemed to come from nowhere. The noise startled all of them.

The Suisamis murmured to each other. Their murmurs turned into a rapid flow of Japanese that communicated alarm in any language. Michael's jaw dropped. Although a storm was coming, seventy-five degrees of balmy air was breezing through the open windows. There was no conceivable reason for the furnace to turn on. Yet every radiator in the place seemed to be turning on all at once, hissing steam, making clanking, clattering noises as if the water shooting through the pipes was hot enough to bust.

Hot water, in fact, spurted out of the far parlor radiator in a geyser at just that moment.

Five

An hour later, the radiators were all cool to the touch. The archaic, two-ton cast-iron Weil-McClain furnace hadn't let out another peep. A few minutes' mopping took care of the water under the radiators. Once that was done, the whole house was idyllically still and peaceful.

Unfortunately the potential customers weren't around to see it. Simone had watched the Suisamis taking off at the speed of sound. At the rpm they were driving, they were conceivably in the hills of Kentucky by now. Ms. Stanford had made pretty fast tracks herself.

"I just don't understand it." Michael plopped the salad bowl onto the table. "The plumber'll be here first thing in the morning, but when I told him on the phone what happened, he said it didn't make any sense, either."

Simone passed him the butter-brushed rolls. "Maybe it was a ghost," she suggested wryly. "Maybe there's a spirit haunting the house who doesn't want you to sell the place."

"You sound like my brothers. Seth, especially, has taken a real liking to that psychic stuff. Not me. I've never found anything that didn't have a logical explanation." He forked a T-bone on her plate. Pink on the inside, not red, and rubbed with fresh pepper. The salad had been her creation, but he'd hot-peppered that, too.

Simone happened to love hot pepper; she just wasn't exactly sure how she ended up sharing a meal with Michael again. There had just come a point when they seemed to be the only players left standing. The hour was past six, and he'd said it was silly for her to have to drive to town and find a place when he had more than enough food around. Simone suspected he hated to eat alone, and how could she just leave him after that crazy debacle with the radiators?

"Well, if you don't buy the idea of our grandparents haunting the place, I'm afraid I don't have another theory," she admitted.

"Your grandmother would have a heck of a time haunting the place, considering she's still alive. And I refuse to talk about those blasted radiators anymore. A couple of hours ago—before all hell broke loose— you started to tell me something. You read one of the diaries, right?"

Simone nodded. It was the first chance she'd had to bring up the subject. "I read the first one, dated 1929. I couldn't believe all the details she put in. It was like being transported to another time."

"Such as...?"

"Such as she saw a movie by a new upstart named Hitchcock—*Blackmail*—and she also saw her first Mickey Mouse film. She liked Mickey Mouse better. She learned to drive on a Model T Ford. Her favorite song was 'Singin' in the Rain,' although Jerome Kern's 'Ol' Man River' had just come out on the radio. She liked that one, too. Prohibition was in. She went to all kinds of speakeasies—not to drink—but because they had music for dancing. Lord, did she love to dance. She lived for it."

Michael cracked open a roll, his eyes on her face. "You expected something different, didn't you? She doesn't sound so wild, Simone. She just sounds... young."

"I *expected* to read the explicit details of a wild, wanton sex life—something along the lines of a Mata Hari rewrite of the Kama Sutra—because those are the kinds of stories Gram always told us. I may kill her when I get home." Simone took a moment to relish that thought. "She never told us anything like this."

"How old was she?"

"Nineteen. A painfully young nineteen. The oldest of five, and her dad lost everything in the crash. She was married to my grandfather three days after Black Thursday by a justice of the peace. My gramps had money. It was as simple as that. I think she believed she was saving her family... and maybe she was." When Michael passed her the rolls, she shook her head regretfully. Carbohydrates like that glued straight to her thighs.

"So... did you find out how she ended up having an affair with my grandfather?"

"No. Not yet. In fact, that was what I couldn't wait to tell you. She met your Benjamin that year. Once.

She not only couldn't stand him on sight—but she gave him a black eye.''

"You're kidding?"

"No." Simone hesitated. "It's real clear that she was unhappy with her marriage from the start. She didn't say anything about her wedding night, but it wasn't hard to figure out that her dancing days were over. She was supposed to stay in the house, wait on him hand and foot, be forever grateful for what he did financially for her family." She hesitated again. "She started sneaking out, going back to those speakeasies when he was away on business. She wasn't doing anything wrong. At least, not then. Except dancing. When she met your Benjamin, he apparently thought she was alone in a bar because she was looking for action. He made a pass. She socked him.''

Michael rolled his eyes. "I have no doubt he deserved it. But it's pretty hard to imagine how they developed a budding romance from that starting point.''

"I'll have to read further to find out. But judging from what I've read so far... I don't know. She's just so different from what I thought. She always told us about her wild escapades, as if she were proud of them, flaunting them. My grandfather died when I was little, so I never really knew him.But I'm afraid he may have been physically abusive. She doesn't exactly say that in the diary, but she just sounds angry and confused and desperately unhappy. She felt trapped. Like she was living in a cage with no escape hatch. And did I tell you she wrote Herbert Hoover about birth control?''

"Run that by me again?"

She chuckled at Michael's disbelieving tone. "It's true. When I first read it, I thought it was funny, too. Can't imagine what the President of the United States thought when he got that letter. But then I thought . . . how desperate could a naive young woman be to feel she had to go that far? She didn't want to bring children into an unhappy marriage. She asked a doctor, her mother, women friends. No one would tell her anything. They just kept lecturing her that it was a woman's role in life to have babies. I have no idea if good old President Hoover wrote her back, but she managed to get herself a diaphragm from somewhere. It was in the next entry."

Michael laid down his fork and rested his arms on the table. "You're glad you found those diaries, aren't you? I can hear the relief in your voice. Your Julia was never so wild or irresponsible. Not like you were afraid of."

"Right now, to be honest, all I feel is confused. She used to say forbidden love is always more fun—as if she climbed into any man's bed who asked her. She was always warning me that I was too serious, that I'd never find love unless I was willing to 'throw caution to the winds' and 'let the romance sing in my soul.'" Simone rubbed two fingers on her temples. "Dammit, Michael. She never let on that she was so unhappy. I feel like a self-righteous prig for always judging her so harshly. And I still can't just accept what she did. No matter what the circumstances, she was still a married woman when she had that affair with your grandfather."

"I think—always did—that you're going to find out my grandfather is the villain in the tale. The kind of bastard who'd seduce a vulnerable woman." Michael fell silent, with the sudden, strangest look of guilt in his eyes, but then he abruptly shook his head with wry, dry humor. "Hell, who knows what you're going to find out? At the moment, our nefarious kin apparently aren't even speaking to each other.''

"I'll get to the next installment in the soap tomorrow."

They both jumped up to tackle the dishes. Simone planned to leave promptly after that. As much as she'd wanted to tell him about the diary, she hadn't expected to spill so many personal feelings. Her grandmother had gotten nothing but trouble by "throwing caution to the winds." Simone had never liked trouble, had always been carefully reticent about exposing her emotions, but sharing with Michael came so easily. He not only understood; he empathized. Maybe that was natural, considering that their grandparents had played a larger-than-life role in both their lives.

But that didn't exactly explain the quick chuckle between them when he dropped a fork. She bumped his hip when she was reaching for a dishcloth, and there was another electric connection. He liked pepper and spices, as she did. He was a fussy, meticulous dish dryer, as she was. They ended up laughing over the silliest coincidental similarities between them, and damn if he didn't have the sexiest eyes on a man she'd ever seen.

By the time she grabbed her purse, her nerves were on a shimmering simmer. It was nothing he did. It was all her fault. Her body had no excuse for turning on. Her slick palms, the feminine awareness thrumming in her pulse, the heat pooling low in her stomach—it was idiocy. Hormones.

When he walked her outside, she dived into her purse for the car keys, yet still couldn't manage to leave. The storm had held off all afternoon, but the skies were a dirty mass of fast-moving clouds now, blocking any hope of a sunset. A restless wind flapped at her skirt hem—any second it was going to rain—yet somehow they were talking again.

"...I caught up with the twins on the phone this morning. Lord, those two are hell on wheels—especially when they're together. One of them broke a window and they're in Dutch with their mother. I got the whole story."

It wasn't the first time Michael had brought up his sons. Usually he relayed some devilish antic they'd gotten into, but Simone could hear the hunger in his voice. He obviously missed them. "I take it they're with their mom while you're here?"

He leaned against the car, his hands shoved into his front pockets. "Carla and I have a cocustody thing. After the divorce, I bought a condo a few miles from the house. Close enough for them to bike the distance. We always do at least one thing during the week, plan something for the weekends." His gaze focused on a pair of gulls, mournfully crying to each other on the rocks. "I hated putting them through the split up, but they seem okay about it. I think we've set it up as good as you're gonna get with a divorce."

He kept staring at those lonesome gulls. She couldn't just leave the conversation hanging there. "You've mentioned Donnie and Davie's reactions before, but what about you? Was the split up pretty rough?"

"It was hard at first. The shock effect, as much as anything else." When he turned back to face her, his eyes were the sharp blue of cut glass. "Carla told me she had to find herself. Hell, I never knew she was lost. Married ten years. I never had the first clue anything was wrong until a guy showed up at my office with the papers. Doesn't say much for how well I knew her, does it?''

Simone wanted to say that it took two to communicate, but she held it back. He wasn't talking about his ex-wife so much as his own feelings. She'd sensed before that the failure of his marriage hung over his head like a glued-on shingle, but not how completely he blamed himself. "It still hurts?" she asked gently.

"In a way," he admitted. "It's over, for sure. I'd never go back to the relationship. But it still bites, that I apparently took for granted what she needed, what mattered to her. I don't think you can fail a lover much worse than that. Maybe I'm just meant to live alone. I'm sure as hell not good with women.''

The wind whipped the hair around her cheeks. She pushed it back, thinking how wonderful he'd been with her, how naturally he seemed to understand her feelings... but Michael surely didn't want to hear that. "Well, I'm no better with men. In fact, I came to the same conclusion— Maybe I'm just meant to live alone. It's not like I've been around a hundred blocks, just a couple. But enough to know that I'm a bad picker. The ski season brings a lot of money, a lot of men looking for a temporary good time. The last one neglected to tell me he was married, and I swear that was the final cruncher. There're plenty of good men out there. It's not them, it's me. My judgment is obviously squee-jawed. I've fallen once too often for the short-distance runners who never intended to stick around—at least not for me.''

"So you put a lock on the heart door?"

"I tend to call it a dead bolt." She smiled. "Sounds like you have, too. We're a hell of a pair, Connor.''

He raised his eyebrows, as if the idea of their being any kind of pair startled him, and then he chuckled. "Maybe that's why I can't seem to stop talking to you? Hell, it's dark. Were you gonna stand there and let me bend your ear all night?"

"You're blaming me?"

"I don't know how to talk to women. That's what I've been trying to tell you, for Pete's sake. It *has* to be your fault."

He pushed away from the car. She lifted her keys. Thunder shuddered in the west, as if reminding both of them how long they'd been standing there. The wind was hurling bits of sand and debris in every direction. He opened the car door for her, and she quickly stepped toward it. It was just an impulse, when she touched his arm. The light of laughter was in his eyes; he was comfortable teasing her. She was comfortable being teased, with this man she barely knew.

But he was more than a stranger now. It weighed on her heart, how wrong he was. Simone took all the blame when a relationship failed, but that was different. She was simply being realistic, where Michael...my Lord, how could he possibly think of himself as a failure with women? He was a woman's dream of a man, honest, warm, a caretaker and protector by nature, a man who empathized and listened and cared. She just couldn't climb into that car and disappear without somehow showing him that she thought he was damn special.

When she touched his arms, though, she couldn't seem to find any words. He cocked his head, as if assuming she wanted to say something, waiting. It was just another impulse, that she bounced up on tiptoe and brushed his cheek. It was meant to be a peck. A gesture of affection. Nothing more. Nothing that should have ignited a maelstrom.

But he turned his head at just that moment, so her lips didn't land on his cheek. They landed on his mouth. In that speck of a second when they were both surprised, the contact had the same dangerous effect as instant glue. They were already... fused.

This kiss wasn't as foreign as their first one. She knew what he tasted like now. She knew the shape and texture of his mouth. She knew she'd gotten into trouble the last time, too, but how could a single innocent match spark such a forest fire?

They were both afraid of repeating past mistakes. Maybe that was the source of the bond? Maybe having Julia and Benjamin in common had created an unusual closeness? Her mind searched for reasons as fruitlessly as those gulls crying on the shore. She didn't feel *reasonable*. She felt as basic as Eve, as if being with Michael peeled down the layers and nothing made sense—nothing had ever made more sense—than the elemental connection of his smooth, warm mouth crushed against hers.

She'd been tired after the long day. She wasn't tired now. His hands closed on her shoulders and tugged her closer. Her senses inhaled him—the ripple of muscles in his chest, the rough catch in his breath, the texture of his rough, whiskered chin. He aroused so fast. One winsome soft kiss was followed by the deep drag of a rough one. He wasn't asking for a response; he was claiming it. She felt his fingertips on her face, on her throat. Yearning spun through her in a spiral of need, hunger, softness—a soul-deep softness pulsing from the pit of her belly. It didn't matter where the feelings came from. They were real. They were bewitching and beguiling and powerful.

A drop of rain splattered on her cheek, so cold it startled her. Michael lifted his head. Fat blops of rain were falling on him, too. The clouds had rustled closer and the darkness crowded in. In the distance she could hear the wild pounding of waves. Before he could swear—she was almost sure he was going to swear—she did it for both of them.

"Dammit, Michael. I'm sorry. I know it had to look like I was coming on to you, but I honestly never meant that to happen."

"It's okay," he said, just as she had the first time this happened. But it was the right tack to take, she thought. The harsh weight of emotion immediately eased in his eyes.

"It's just sex. Like you said before."

"Yeah," he agreed.

"We already knew we were attracted. We were already honest about it, so it's not like we have to deny those feelings exist. It's just . . . I guess we need to be more careful."

"Yeah," he agreed.

"And that shouldn't be hard. We're both practical people. We're both too old to believe in *romance* or anything silly like that. Neither of us wants anything complicated to happen. We understand each other."

"Exactly," Michael said.

"There ain't a thing wrong with her. Godfrey mighty, these old Weil-McClains were built to last forever. Not real energy efficient by today's standards, mind you—bet it costs a fortune to heat this old place—but she's sound as a dollar."

Michael frowned. A phone rang in the other room, which he ignored, knowing the answering machine would get it. The plumber's name was George Wiley; he was a big burly man with the face of a bassett hound, not the ears, but definitely the hangdog jowls. "Are you telling me there's no reason why the radiators would suddenly turn on?"

"Oh, ayuh. Sure enough there's an explanation—somebody musta flicked the switch on a thermostat. But you called me out to find if there was something wrong with the furnace. Ain't nothing wrong." George hiked up his belt over a watermelon-size girth and squinted at him amiably. "If you don't turn on the furnace in the middle of July, you won't have a problem."

Michael pinched the bridge of his nose. George was something of a character. His speech was peppered with northeastern mannerisms—he agreed to have a "squid" of coffee, threw in oaths such as 'godfrey mighty,' and clearly believed that *AH* was the alphabet letter between *q* and *s*. Communicating with him had been an interesting trial, particularly since George refused to take the problem seriously. "I'm telling you that no one was near any of the thermostats. There aren't any thermostats in the parlor. And we were all in the same room."

"Well, somebody had to brush up against a switch, chum. That's the only explanation there is." George picked up his toolbox and started lumbering for the back door. "'Course, there is one other answer. Lot of people in these parts say your house is haunted."

He waited. Michael repressed an exasperated sigh. Probably that was how his brothers had picked up that psychic nonsense—some Mainer getting a tickle from putting on an "outsider." "I haven't bought a wooden nickle in this decade," he said flatly.

"Well, now, that's my view, too. But there's a lot of tales about that ghost. A pirate, they say. A buccaneer from Revolutionary War Times. Don't set my clock by such stories, myself, but you go down to Freezie's on a Tuesday night, now, there's some old-timers who'd tell you some tales."

"Thanks, but I pass," Michael said dryly.

George looked disappointed the outsider hadn't bitten. He squinted at the check Michael had written him. "Well, now, you be sure to call me if you have any other problems. Don't you even hesitate."

"Thanks for the offer. I appreciate your coming out so quickly."

"Ayeh. Was no bother. Were you out earlier this morning? The roads were sure greezy after last night's rain...."

George was willing to chatter all day. It took another few minutes before Michael could shoo him out and close the back door. Hands on his hips, he watched the battered red pickup back out of the driveway, then aimed for the bubbling pot on the stove.

He'd been mainlining caffeine all morning, but it wasn't doing any good. He hadn't slept. A telephone call came in at two in the morning—one of the plants, a press breakdown. After that he couldn't settle down, thinking about his sons. Thinking about his brothers. Thinking about the plumber coming this morning, and the house buyers Paula had lined up the next day, and what the *hell* he was going to do if this albatross didn't sell.

And yeah, thinking about Simone.

He poured the black liquid into a mug, closed his eyes and took a long pull.

"If I'd known ye were calling that man, I'd have told ye, lad. There was no need. 'Twas me caused the problem. I had to do something. 'Tis your house, and those other people didna belong."

The coffee sputtered out of his mouth. Michael's eyes popped open. The sunlit kitchen was empty, the only sounds the ticking of the clock and the coffeepot hissing on the stove. He'd heard it several times now—the man's voice with the Scottish accent—but of course, there was no one there. Unlike his brothers, he couldn't be less susceptible to such psychic nonsense.

Impatiently, carrying the mug, he crossed the room toward the hall. The plumber had taken up two hours of the morning; Simone was due after lunch; and he had serious work to do while the house was quiet.

His heels clicked on the chestnut floor. A shadow blurred in the long antique mirror as he passed it. His own, he was sure.

"She'll be over again, I'm hopin'? I sat with her yesterday in the blue bedroom. I didna scare her, not to worry, but a man canna help but look. She's a winsome lassie. More than winsome. I've always been a good judge of women. In my time, Blackbeard—his real name was Edward Teach—they said he was the one good with the lassies. Not as good as meself, though. I ken tell with one look if a woman is gonna be good between the sheets...."

Michael pushed open the library door. The fax was noisily spewing out messages. The answering machine button was flashing. The damn room was laser-bright, took all the morning sun, and there was a perfectly rational reason why he was hearing that voice. How many millions of articles had he read on insomnia? None of them were a lick of help. But anyone who suffered sleep deprivation long enough could undergo some perfectly understandable symptoms. Blurred vision. A little fanciful imagination. It wasn't *insanity* or anything unnerving like that; the problem would disappear as soon as the sufferer got some sleep.

"...I ken picture her curled around ye in the night. The gold hair on yer pillow, her naked in yer arms. I knew her grandmother years ago. She's like her Julia. Both a type to take the world on their shoulders, afraid to love, afraid to believe in love...but a strong, aggressive man can show her what love can be. Ye already know what moves her. I saw ye kissing her outside the house last night...."

Michael dropped into the desk chair and zapped on the computer. Color promptly flashed on the monitor—welcome, normal, civilized, electronic color. Everything was fine. Although his insomnia was chronic, he was temporarily experiencing the roughest patch he'd ever had. In that sense it was perfectly logical that he was suffering a few symptoms. Even the context was logical. Imagining Simone, in bed with him, making love with him, coming apart in his arms, was certainly part of the reason he'd given up sleep and taken to pacing half the night.

"...She's crazy for ye, lad. She's hot for ye. I ken tell, I know these things. She's a loving woman. She's got feelings bottled up inside, just waiting for the right man to turn them loose. Ye could make her burn. 'Twouldna be that difficult, and I know ye've had trouble sleeping. I'd wager you'd sleep like a newborn babe after making love with her...."

There was a message on the screen from Roberta. Seven of them, actually. Michael considered the questions and problems she'd asked, reached for the coffee cup and then meticulously put it down. His system begged for the caffeine—*damn,* he was tired—but possibly the mixture of caffeine and sleeplessness was adding to the problem. Not the problem of the stupid voice. The problem, the relentless, chugging, thought train in his head, about Simone.

No woman had ever whipped his hormones into such a fervor. He was a rational, careful, sensible man. He ran his life by rules. And maybe he was hopeless at understanding women, but he'd never taken advantage of any. Never hurt one by choice. And he'd certainly never been like his grandfather, preying on the vulnerable and susceptible of the species.

Simone was vulnerable. Michael would have liked to kick the sonsofguns who'd taken her for a ride—kick them straight to Poughkeepsie—but she had it all wrong about being "bad with men." Her judgment wasn't the problem. Men were. It was inevitable that she'd run across some bastards—she was damned beautiful, clearly tended toward trusting, and was feminine to the core. The same softness that made her irresistible to a man was always going to make her vulnerable to the real ruthless types.

"...Her skin, lad, did ye ever see skin that irresistibly soft? Reminds ye of a morning mist on the sea. Just to touch that skin could arouse a devil hunger in a man, I'm thinking. One touch, one taste, wouldna be enough, tho. I think ye already discovered that, haven't ye? Should ye need coaching in seduction techniques, now, I'd be more than happy to help ye...."

Michael switched off the computer, washed a hand over his face and closed his eyes. Bewilderment spun through him. It was not a familiar emotion. His attitude toward Simone should be cut-and-dried— It wasn't as if he'd forgotten how completely he'd failed his ex-wife. No man could save himself from making mistakes, but he could sure as hell make sure he didn't repeat his failures. It was obviously wisest for him to avoid women—and especially women who threw him curve balls.

Simone could put a tailspin on a straight pitch. There were two women inside that blond head—the pragmatic realist who wore tailored clothes and claimed total cynicism about romance...and the soft-eyed temptress who responded to him as if he was the hottest lover who'd ever come down the pike. It was like having puzzle pieces that didn't fit. Michael had no idea what she really needed, what she really wanted, only the needle-sharp instinct that the man who cared about her had *better* know. The kind of guy who'd bungle around her sensitive feelings could hurt her badly. He was that bungler type. According to Carla, he'd aced the course in insensitivity. Bewilderment was no excuse—not when his only option was as plain as peanut butter.

He had to leave her alone.

Six

Head buried, her fanny in the air, Simone burrowed deeper into the steamer trunk. Assorted debris was piled next to her. So far she'd come up with veils and hats, three bud vases, a book of poetry and a variety of French lingerie. All of it was fascinating but not, right now, what she was searching for.

She dived deeper. There! Her fingers connected with satin fabric. Slowly, carefully, she pulled out the dress for a better look. There was light in the attic now. Days before, when Michael figured out she was spending more time in the attic than the blue bedroom, he'd hauled up a floor fan and a pair of lanterns. The whirl of the fan blades was the only sound in that shadowy corner under the eaves, and the soft lantern light glowed on the lustrous satin—causing a catch in her throat.

The dress had originally been white, Simone knew from the diary entry, but the color had faded to a pale yellow, and the fabric was hopelessly wrinkled. Still, she couldn't seem to stop staring at it. She couldn't seem to stop... touching it.

The style was shamelessly simple. Slim shoulder straps dipped to a low, loose bodice and then simply dropped to a handkerchief hem. The soft, light satin was as wicked and revealing as a nightgown. Seductive. Sensuous. Sultry. It was a dress for a romantic dreamer, a dress for a woman who had the guts to embrace her own sensuality, a dress for a blatant femme fatale.

Yet her grandmother had been none of those things. A restless shiver chased down her spine, thinking of all the brassy advice Julia had fed her over the years: Throw caution to the winds! Let the romance sing in your soul! And Simone knew what she'd expected when she read the diaries—a sordid little tale of a married woman's unconscionable affair.

But she'd read two more years of entries now. She knew exactly how the relationship between the lovers had developed. And nothing, absolutely nothing, was what she'd anticipated. Her grandmother had never been loose, never been any wild femme fatale. Those tales had been nothing more than talk. She'd simply been a scared, lonely and desperately unhappy young woman when she'd met Benjamin. And he'd taught her... joy. An emotion she had no experience with. An emotion she'd never expected to feel.

Simone stroked the soft fabric, feeling disturbed and increasingly confused. All her life, she'd been afraid of becoming like Julia—the kind of woman that a man used and took advantage of. She'd never expected to identify with Julia, much less to discover that her grandmother had been wary of love, distrustful of romance, scared of trusting her own feelings . . . exactly, too damn much, just like her.

The dress seemed a symbol of the only difference between them. Simone may have made mistakes, but she'd never thrown away the rigid rule book. Julia had. Julia had been scared to death when she first wore that dress, but she'd swallowed her fears and taken the risk and reached out—for Benjamin. Simone tried to imagine what kind of love would give a woman the nerve, the freedom to expose her vulnerability in a dress like this one.

On the spur of an impulse—a really *stupid* impulse—Simone pulled her oversize blue T-shirt over her head. She got up to check the attic door—it was closed; Michael was surely busy downstairs—yet she still felt silly and foolish when she peeled off her shorts. She'd only try it on for a second. She'd take it right off. It probably wouldn't fit and she'd undoubtedly look ridiculous— She'd never be the type to pull off "white slink" in this lifetime. She just wanted to understand how her grandmother had felt.

But Lord, it fit. The satin rippled over her head, shimmied and shivered over her bare skin. Sin had never felt this wicked. As she could have guessed, the dress revealed every embarrassing flaw in her figure— small breasts, too-plump hips. Yet her reflection in the cracked, wavery mirror in the shadows still startled her. The woman staring back at her was standing straight and proud, with silver-gold hair whispering on her bare shoulders and a sleepy sensuality in her eyes. It was the satin, Simone told herself. Probably any woman would look and feel differently wearing nothing but satin next to her skin.

Her grandmother had worn a camellia in her hair. She'd pressed the flower, saved it. And no jewelry, just a white satin ribbon like a choker. She'd saved that, too, according to the diary, but it took Simone several minutes to find both the ribbon and the camellia.

She never heard the attic door open. If the whirling fan hadn't muffled all sound, she would surely have heard him climbing the wooden steps. Michael was holding two glasses of lemonade and had been standing there heaven knew for how long. It was the chink of melting ice cubes in those glasses that made her suddenly realize she wasn't alone.

He was wearing a collarless shirt and khakis, and he seemed to have forgotten his purpose in bringing the lemonade. The light at the stairs was so dim that his expression was shadowed, but she could still see his eyes, lucent and dark, focused on her, arrested on her in that dress.

When he realized she'd spotted him, he stepped up the last stair and cleared his throat. "I . . . didn't mean to interrupt whatever you were doing. You'd just been up here so many hours that I thought you might want a break."

"You didn't interrupt. Or you did, but I . . . *damn.* Nobody's caught me doing anything this embarrassing since I was about six." An iceberg couldn't have cooled the fire shooting up her cheeks. "Talk about feeling colossally silly. You *know* I'm not the romantic type. I don't even know what possessed me to try on this old stuff—"

"I take it the dress was your grandmother's?"

"Yes." Michael had looked at her before in a way that made her heart stutter and thump. But not like this. She wished she had miles and pounds of blankets to cover herself. For a few crazy moments, the damn dress had made her feel like a different woman. The kind of woman she'd never been, could never be. Her hand shot up to yank the camellia out of her hair.

"Don't. Leave it there," Michael said swiftly. "You look beautiful, Simone."

"Did you break into the whiskey after lunch?" she asked suspiciously.

"No. But I'm tempted to have one now." His gaze slow-danced the length of her. "If your Julia looked anything remotely like you, I may take back every bad thing I ever said or thought about my grandfather. Hell, he had justifiable motivation for committing murder and mayhem."

"Michael, quit teasing. But as far as my grand-mother—she really was extraordinarily pretty. Noth-ing like me." She didn't want to move, knowing the satin displayed every sway, every movement, maybe even every heartbeat. But she couldn't very well strip off the dress with him there. So she covered her nerves by quickly handing him a tarnished-silver picture frame. "My grandmother said the photo was taken in 1931 with the 'new natural color photography.' The quality sure isn't Kodak and it's really faded now—but it's the only picture I found of the two of them."

Michael set down both glasses of lemonade on a trunk, then raised the photo up to the lantern light. He studied it a moment, then looked back at her. "The likeness is almost eerie. You have her eyes, her hair color. But I can't imagine where you got the idea she was prettier than you. She doesn't hold a candle."

"You're just trying to make me feel less...foolish."

"Actually, I was trying to make you feel good—and apparently failing abysmally, which is no surprise. Never once in my life have I ever managed to say the right thing around a woman. If it makes you feel uncomfortable to be told you look beautiful, I take it all back. You look terrible. You look horrible. Is that better? Now, are you gonna tell me the latest installment in our wicked relatives' love lives, or keep me holding my breath?"

She started to chuckle. She couldn't help it. Michael kept claiming to have no perception about women. But what other man would, deadpan, tell a woman that she looked horrible solely to make her feel less self-conscious? And it worked. She forgot about how she was dressed, perched on the edge of a trunk and just...talked with him. "Michael—I found out about this house. How they got together. Everything."

"Yeah?" He handed her a glass of lemonade. "So far, I haven't a clue how they ended up having an affair. The last I knew, your grandmother had the good sense to sock my grandfather."

"Well, since then, I've read two more years of diaries. 1930 and 1931. She filled in all these details about what was happening in the times...like Robert Frost published one of his volumes of collected poems. And somebody named Tombaugh discovered the planet Pluto. People were starting to talk about Freud and his theories. Marlene Dietrich had a smash hit in *The Blue Angel* and everyone was singing 'Georgia On My Mind.' In 1931, the 'Star-Spangled Banner' became the national anthem. But that was the fun stuff...."

Simone took another long sip of lemonade. "By 1931, there were twelve million people out of work, on the breadlines. The Depression affected everyone by then. My Julia's family especially. Her marriage had gone from bad to worse—he was physically abusive when he drank—but she was as trapped as a cooked goose. She was afraid of him, but even more afraid that her family would starve if she got a divorce. If she didn't occasionally get out of the house, she was afraid she'd lose her mind.''

''So she snuck out, like before?'' Michael guessed.

Simone nodded. ''She went dancing. And that's where she kept running into your Benjamin. He came back—even after she'd socked him—and when she wanted to dance, he was there. Frankly, I think he was protecting her, Michael. Any man could have hit on her, being alone like that. And he didn't make any more passes, not for over a year. He told her honestly that he was separated from his wife, but he didn't know if there would ever be a divorce because she was Catholic. He wasn't looking for trouble, just an occasional few hours with someone to talk to. He no longer believed in love, he told Julia. She no longer believed in love, either, she told him.''

Simone gestured. ''Michael...I honestly don't think they meant anything serious to happen. All they did was dance. Neither thought that was so wrong. My grandmother was so young. She had no one in her life to just laugh with, talk with, have *fun* with.'' She sighed. ''Anyway, it was stifling hot that summer in Colorado. She had friends in Maine, left over from the times she'd vacationed there as a child. Her husband said she could spend a month there—probably because he knew the people, and had to be away on business himself.''

''The plot thickens?'' Michael murmured.

"Exactly. When she got to the East Coast, Benjamin showed up. I'd guess he was already in love with her by then, Michael, even if my grandmother didn't realize it. She said she couldn't go out with him. However innocent their meetings had been to that point, they'd been discreet. No one knew. Benjamin told her he'd find a place. Just a place where they could dance. She thought he meant some little obscure restaurant."

"Don't tell me. That's when he bought this house?"

Simone nodded. "She was...overwhelmed. But he hadn't laid a finger on her, Michael. At least not at the end of 1931, which is as far as I finished reading. They were both still swearing that they were never going to have an affair. But do you know what your wretch of a grandfather gave her?"

"No, what?"

"A pot of four-leaf clovers," Simone said glumly.

Michael looked totally mystified. "Clovers?"

"Her husband had the money to buy her jewels. And your damn Benjamin sat in some damn field and actually took the time to find a whole pot of four-leaf clovers, just for her. Now how was she supposed to resist that?"

Michael cleared his throat. "I take it you think that was a...reprehensible thing for him to do?"

"I think it was unbearably sentimental. Lord. The two of them were hopeless romantics. Not an ounce of common sense or judgment between them." Simone shook her head. "Thank heavens, we're nothing like them."

Michael's gaze drifted from the dress to the camellia to the velvet ribbon at her throat. "Thank heavens," he echoed.

"My grandmother always said I was too much of a practical realist."

His eyes wandered to the debris surrounding her—the Victorian frame, the scraps of pressed flowers and lace, the poetry books. "My family always complained I was a hard-headed realist, too."

"Nothing like that could ever happen to us," Simone said with a sigh of relief.

"No way," Michael agreed.

He wasn't falling for her. That wasn't possible. This recent, unreasonable obsession he had with Simone had an obvious source. Most women confused him, but Simone . . . hell, she took the blue ribbon in totally and completely bewildering him.

The telephone jingled. He ignored it. The fax screeched an incoming message. He paid no attention. Simone said she'd be by this afternoon, and any minute now, Paula Stanford was supposed to bring another group to look at the house. He didn't budge. Through the narrow tall windows behind the desk, he had a prize view of the sloping lawn that led to the beach. The landscaping people were due to cut it the next day. Right now, though, the grass was a verdant, thick, lush green. There had to be weeds in it, he thought. Wasn't clover some form of weed?

Michael scraped a hand through his hair. He just didn't get it—why a woman would go all dreamy-eyed over weeds? Even less could he fathom how a woman could label herself a practical realist—straight to his face yet—when she was clearly a sucker for camellias and love stories and yeah, four-leaf clovers.

The vision of her in that white dress still made his throat go dry. When he'd come up the stairs, she'd been looking in the mirror as she pinned on the camellia. Her lips were parted, her cheeks were vividly flushed, and those damn eyes of hers had a shy, soft, yearning glow.

She'd been on tiptoe, stretching this way and that, trying to see how the dress looked. He could have told her. The satin draped her body like a man's private fantasy. The fabric peeked at her breasts, nipped at her long waist, snuggled closer than a lover's hand over her fanny, and made his temperature rise ten degrees in five seconds flat.

Simone hadn't guessed how he felt. He'd acted normal, hadn't he? For one brief, insane instant, he'd been tempted to sweep her into his arms and slow-dance her the length of the attic. She'd been humming "Georgia on My Mind." Undoubtedly his grandfather would have given in to the romantic impulse with his Julia— but Michael wasn't his grandfather. And naturally, he'd done no such thing.

He slugged his hands into his pockets and jiggled his change. Everything was normal. Nothing had changed. For the last three nights, he'd had a particularly nasty bout with insomnia. Lack of sleep was undoubtedly the reason he was hearing ghosts, the reason he lay awake thinking—shamefully, inexcusably imagining—Simone in his bed. Him, playing the role of the romantic forbidden lover. Her, skimming that white satin dress over her head and coming to him naked by moonlight.

Michael scowled. Even insomnia was no excuse for a man to lose his wits. Simone wasn't looking for a lover—and if she were, it would never be him. For the first time in his life, he'd found a woman he could be honest with. They were pals. He'd never had a woman pal before, and damned if he was going to blow it. They'd both acknowledged the sizzle of chemistry between them—even a few kisses had been a trial by fire. But she'd said what she wanted. Peace. A no-hurt stretch of time. She wasn't up to the risk of failing in another relationship right now.

Since her no-involvement program matched his own fears of failing in another relationship—he'd believed her. It never occurred to him *not* to believe her...except for the way she looked at him. Except for the way she was with him. Except for the confoundedly mystifying romantic side to her nature that kept sneaking up to the surface.

Outside, a silky summer wind ruffled the lawn. Squinting hard, he hung out over the sill, almost positive he saw some rounded shapes mingled in the straight shafts of grass. Hell, it could take a man hours—it could take a man *weeks*—to find an entire potful of four-leaf clovers.

The doorbell rang. He jumped, then abruptly slammed the window closed and hustled down the hall. Sanity was arriving—thank God.

Michael didn't care who Paula was bringing to look at the house, as long as it sold. The sooner this monster was out of his hair, the sooner he could go home, back to safety, back to his sons and his work and his whole rational, normal life. Trouble. He couldn't shake the feeling that the longer he stayed in this damn house, the more he risked getting into confounding, serious trouble.

He yanked open the front door...to find more trouble.

Ms. Stanford wore a screaming red-and-yellow print that was certainly designed to rivet a man's attention. All he noticed were the car doors slamming in his driveway. "I told you I was bringing a family," Paula said, "but possibly I should have asked you ahead of time if you had any objection to children—"

"Are you kidding? Why would you possibly think I'd object to children? This house is ideal for kids...."

A van was parked behind Paula's car, but he didn't particularly notice that, either. Simone had just pulled in, and she was really the only one he saw. She stepped out of her blue compact with a satchel of diaries in her arms. She was wearing white. Just a cool rayon shirt and shorts, nothing like that white dress she'd worn the other afternoon, but the sun caught the silvery-gold sheen of her hair. As before, her throat was bare. As before, the stark white color made him think of virginal untapped innocence when, impossibly, no color on her could have been sexier. The contrast to her peach-soft skin and dark eyes was alluringly sensual and disturbingly striking.

Their eyes met. For him, she had a smile. One of *those* smiles, that could make a man stupidly believe she was uniquely, privately glad to see him. His heart pedaled double time. Since there was no explaining why a grown man would react to the simple look of a woman that way, he'd given up trying. When she chuckled suddenly, though, he turned his head.

The doors to the tan van were all open, and children were pelting out. Not a couple of kids. Not a few kids. But an entire swarm. He counted eleven streaking past him—most of them carrot tops with facefuls of freckles—before he raised startled eyes to Paula.

"There's an even dozen of the little monsters," Paula said under her breath. "You can surely see why they need a big house. Financing might be a slight problem, but at the price you're giving away the property, I believe the O'Briens can handle it."

He didn't have the time to worry about it, nor could he catch a moment alone with Simone. She probably meant to disappear from sight and head up to the attic, but the children were a tad diverting. He caught her scooping up one devil-eyed urchin as he slid down the banister, and saving another of the younger models who was trying to climb a highboy in the parlor.

Entertaining a pack of wild wolves had to be easier. The turret room was an echo chamber for high-pitched screams. The upstairs hall thundered with the creaks and groans of a relay race . Simone appeared one other time, her face flushed, laughter in her eyes as she claimed the key to the library which—holy spit!—he should have thought of locking himself. He wasn't exactly sure how he ended up holding a wet-diapered thumb sucker, but the baby draped on his neck was at least quiet. The O'Brien couple were apparently used to communicating at symphonic sound levels. He answered questions about furnaces, property taxes, electric bills, water. At least he thought he did.

They stuck around for more than three hours. Michael was a little frazzled, but he really didn't care if they stayed for three days—not once he realized they were serious about buying the place. They were obviously totally in love with it. The deal was going down. He could sense it, smell it. Mr. O'Brien, in fact, was covering nitty-gritty financing terms with Paula when they all heard an incredibly weird sound coming from the kitchen.

The house had been filled with endless discordant sounds for hours, of course, but this was distinctly different. The adults stopped talking, looked at each other, and then rushed toward the kitchen.

There wasn't a soul in there. Not even one of the kids. Yet the cupboard doors were all open and flapping, slamming back on their hinges as if a tornado wind were gusting through the kitchen. Only there was no tornado wind. Outside it was a misty sunny day, with a summer breeze so light that he could hear the coos and cries of cheerful bird song from the windows. Michael stared dumbfoundedly at the wildly slamming cupboards. Mrs. O'Brien didn't. With a little shriek, she snatched the baby out of his arms, and in sixty seconds flat had herded her entire pack out the front door. Paula Stanford threw up her hands. "I'll talk to you *later*," she said with exasperation, and took off after her customers.

The van peeled out of the driveway, with Paula's car riding on their tail. Michael was still standing in the doorway when Simone sidled up next to him.

"I don't suppose," she said calmly, "that you have the first clue what just happened?"

He saw the suspicious gleam in her eyes. "Don't you *dare* laugh, Hartman. Dammit, that's the second set of customers we had straight in the bag. And no, I don't have a clue what happened—but I'm sure as hell going to find out."

Seven

Michael made a call from the telephone extension in the kitchen. There was no answer at Seth's, but his youngest brother was home and responded by the third ring. Michael didn't waste his breath on extensive greetings. "Dammit, Zach. What the *hell* is with this house? And I don't want to hear any ribbing or teasing or idiotic psychic stuff. I need some answers, and I need them *now*."

On the other end, Zach—the one brother who could always be counted on for tactful sensitivity and a sympathetic listening ear—burst out laughing. "Don't tell me. You've found a woman and you're in love."

Like an unwilling magnet, Michael's gaze whipped to Simone. She hadn't heard. She was ambling around the room, quietly closing all the gaping cupboard doors. The sun drenched her cheek and throat with light when she passed the window. His eyes riveted on her face and lingered. She'd stayed cool through the commotion and confusion; she'd been there for him—not for the first time. Nothing seemed to shake her except, strangely, kisses from him.

Kisses from her had the disturbing habit of shaking him the same way. He hadn't put a name on why. Labeling a four-letter word like "love" was dangerous. Damning his brother for putting impossible ideas in his head, Michael abruptly washed a hand over his face and clapped the receiver closer to his ear. "Don't try to sidetrack me, Zach. The only thing I'm calling about is this house. I'm talking about a furnace that suddenly turns on in the middle of a warm summer day. I'm talking about cupboard doors swinging open and closed for no reason. I'm talking about too many damn things around here that don't make a lick of sense."

This information seemed to fly right past his brother's head. "I understand. You probably can't talk about her if she's right there. Hell, I can't wait to talk to Seth. We both told you the house had magic, didn't we?"

Michael rolled his eyes. "Okay, forget it. Just let me talk to Kirstin. Your wife, thank God, is at least grounded in reality. *She'll* tell me what's going on—"

"Michael?"

"*What?*" Michael waited, but his brother fell silent for a long ten seconds. When Zach finally started talking, his voice was heavyweight serious.

"Forget about Carla. I know you never saw her as selfish or self-centered, but Seth and I sure did. We never said anything because hell, for a long time we thought you were happy. But I'm telling you now. She was a prize witch. If you've got a chance at the brass ring, I hope you've got the sense to grab it with both fists.''

Long after Michael severed the connection, he found himself staring blankly at the telephone.

"What'd he say?" Simone asked.

Slowly he hung up the receiver. "Nothing I was expecting to hear in a thousand years." He glanced quickly at Simone. "But nothing, unfortunately, that had anything to do with the house."

She cocked her head curiously. "But he was here, right? Not long ago?"

"Yeah, both my brothers were here—Zach, last fall, and Seth in the spring. Both claimed there were some strange goings-on in this house, but since ribbing me is one of their favorite pastimes, I just thought they were joking."

"And now?"

"And now, damned if I know. The more I talk with my brothers, the less sure I am about anything." His gaze lingered on her face again, as if her soft eyes and sweet mouth had answers. Maybe they did. He was unsettlingly sure he wanted to be with her, no matter why or where. "It's past six," he said abruptly. "Any chance I could interest you in dinner and a fool's mission?"

"A fool's mission?" she echoed humorously.

"I'm afraid you'd put me in a straitjacket if I tried to explain. Hell, I'm beginning to think I'm ready for a straitjacket anyway. Have you ever heard of a local place called Freezie's?"

"No."

Michael sighed. "This could well be a classic bad idea, but what the hey. I'm starving and I'll bet you are, too. And from what I heard, there's at least a slim, remote chance that the place might be interesting."

Interesting was an understatement, Simone mused an hour later. The place wasn't located far from Bar Harbor, but it was definitely off the beaten tourist track. Understandably they passed it twice. The weathered, faded sign was hanging from one hinge, and the clapboard building was almost completely concealed behind a nest of bushy pines. The owner obviously wasn't concerned about attracting customers.

Once inside, Simone could see why— The place was packed. The menu was posted on a wall. Bean-hole beans and clam fritters were the night's special. A varnished pine bar gleamed in the dim light. The place was crammed with booths and wooden tables and smelled of tobacco smoke, whiskey and testosterone. The men were all ages, wearing a range of styles from sleeveless T's to worn plaid shirts. Simone didn't see any women. Her white rayon blouse and slacks wouldn't have attracted attention anywhere else, but a dozen pairs of male eyes pounced on her the instant she walked in.

She felt Michael's protective hand at the small of her back. "About the last thing I was expecting was an all-male bar," he muttered. "If you're going to feel uncomfortable, we'll split right now."

"No, really, it's fine with me," she assured him. She wasn't about to leave without discovering why he'd wanted to come here. And it wasn't as if the bar were rough. It just looked like a place where fishermen hung out after a long day's work. "Nobody's likely to bother us. You're not as familiar with Mainers as I am. They notoriously think of tourists as 'summer complaints.' No one's going to pay any attention to a couple of strangers."

By the time the bartender served them a pitcher of foaming beer and a platter of clam fritters, Simone acknowledged that she was dead wrong. Everyone in the place had noticed Michael. Initially she thought the covert glances and swiftly turned heads were for the obvious reason. Michael didn't flaunt anything about himself, but in a pack of men, he was always going to stand out. He met the eyes of one bearded man who was studiously looking her over. The guy dropped his eyes faster than lead-weight stones and didn't look again.

"Remind me to take you with me if I ever have to walk down a dark alley," she murmured.

"Pardon?"

"Nothing. I was just wondering if you realized how many of the men seemed to... well, recognize you. Do you know some of these people?"

Humor lines crinkled at the corners of his eyes. "Honey—trust me—it isn't me drawing their attention. If I ever bring you here again, I'm gonna make you wear sackcloth and a babushka." His gaze riveted on her face. "Actually I don't think even that would help."

She shied away from the compliment, although she could feel her cheeks flushing. "Babushka?"

"Isn't that the name for one of those scarf things? Babushka? Schamooshka? Something like that?"

He'd teased her with compliments before, but something was different tonight. Ever since he'd talked to his brother on the phone, Simone had the odd feeling that Michael was wrestling something on his mind. She wasn't so egotistical to think it was *her*, but he kept studying her in a way that made her skin feel warm and her senses acutely aware of him. Silliness? Heaven knew, they were just talking.

"Tell me about this partner you work with. You said it was a man?"

She nodded. "John Walther is his name. He's about sixty, an old ski pro—even competed in the Olympics years ago. He developed a line of ski equipment, expensive stuff but state of the art for people serious about the sport. When he found me, he'd opened the store but it was floundering financially. He knows his product, just had too many wild marketing ideas, and he took me on as a partner. As he put it, he needed someone who was practical about business, sensible, long on common sense."

"Like you," Michael murmured quietly.

There was the most curious expression in his eyes, but she couldn't read it. "Like me," she agreed.

"Do most people who know you see you that way? Practical, sensible, long in the common sense department?"

"Well...sure. I'm not likely to take off on a wild hair or believe in buried treasure," she said with a smile. "Neither are you, I think."

"No." Michael took a sip of beer. "We're alike. I've never once considered taking a risk on buried treasure before."

"Before? Before what?"

The conversation had taken another odd turn, she thought. Michael seemed to weigh everything she said as if there were some hidden meaning she was missing. But he didn't answer her question— He didn't have a chance.

By that time, they'd both finished dinner and the bartender had whisked away the dishes. Under the table, she'd slipped off her shoes and curled a leg under her, so absorbed in talking with Michael that she'd forgotten there were other people in the bar—until an old gentleman with a chin full of white whiskers ambled over with a cane to stand in front of their booth.

"You're the one living in the Connor house, aren't you?"

Michael automatically extended a hand. "Yes. I'm Michael Connor, and you're—?"

"Rayne Ferguson. My family's been running lobsters in this area for generations. I know your house. Wondered if you'd run across Jock."

"Jock?"

Mr. Ferguson pulled up a chair and ordered them another pitcher of ale. Simone didn't mind the intrusion—the gregarious old man was quite a character and obviously lonely for someone to chitchat with—but she was a little startled when he settled down and started spinning ghost yarns.

"Ghosts all through Maine, now, always have been. We've got our Footless Ghost of Benton Falls, the 'Flying Dutchman of Maine,' and Freeport's always had her haunted tavern. Our pirate ghosts are the most infamous, though, and your Jock sure ain't the only one. The islands of Casco Bay stretch from South Portland to the mouth of the Kennebec River. One of those islands named Jewell was a hideout for Captain Kidd in the 1600s. He hid treasure on Jewell, they say. Some reports claim he bequeathed his treasure map on his death bed, which I personally think must have been difficult, considering he died hung by a noose and never had a deathbed." Mr. Ferguson popped his suspenders in appreciation of his own wit. "Anyhoo. That end of the island, where he was supposed to have bur-

ied his treasure, there been eerie lights and strange
sounds after dark ever since. Some seen a bluish glow
from a mysterious light. Islanders have heard screams
and groans and women's cries.''

The old man paused for effect with a glance at Simone. "And then there's your Jock. He ain't that scary
a ghost, you want the truth. 'Twas his house back in
the 1700s. He built it for the lady he loved, set her up
there and she'd pace that widow's walk waiting for him
while he took off on his thieving, buccaneering ways.
Didn't have a moral to his name. Loved a fight, loved
the sea, would slay any man who crossed him, but he
had a real soft spot for love.''

"Love?'' Simone echoed.

"Ayuh. Two hundred years of legends about him.
The house changed hands a dozen times, but the tales
about him were always of a like. Jock likes lovers, he
does. A girl in trouble, a man having problems wooing his girl, lovers what can't get together— That's
when Jock makes himself known. You can ask a lot of
people in these parts; they'll tell you the same thing.
Nothing to be afraid of, you understand. He's not the
kind of spirit to harm a soul. But it's a dangerous house
for a single man to stay in, and that's for sure.'' The old
man shot them a rheumy, sly glance. "'Course, mebbe
you two are already in love and don't need to worry
about ol' Jock.''

It was past eleven when they left the bar. The night
had turned ebony-black, with a velvet fog shrouding
the trees in mist. Michael hooked an arm around her
shoulder as they walked to the car. She lifted her head.
"Did you know ahead of time that we'd run into
something like that?''

"There was no way I expected a storyteller like Ferguson, but the plumber told me about the place. He said there was a crowd that hung out there who were into local ghost stories, so I had the feeling—at least I hoped—we might hear some ghost lore. Did you enjoy it?"

"More than enjoyed. It was great fun." They both climbed into the car and strapped seat belts. Michael's sleek black New Yorker started with a purr. Once he backed out, his headlights shot like beacons on the deserted road. "So...do you think the problems you've had are because good old Jock is haunting your house?"

"I think a big old house like that deserves a legend or two connected with it. Hell, the story of a matchmaking ghost could probably help sell it."

"But you're not about to believe it yourself?" She smiled so he'd know she was teasing, but truthfully when the old man had been spinning tales, she'd felt more than one silly shiver snake up her spine.

"I believe old houses come with creaks and groans and spooky sounds. Things happen when an old house settles. Add an ocean site and a deserted lighthouse for atmosphere, and even a nonbeliever might be tempted to believe in spirits."

There was something in his tone that made her pause. "Michael...*you're* not seriously tempted to believe, are you?"

"We're both too rational and logical to believe in anything like that, aren't we?"

"I...of course we are." They were very much alike. That kindred spirit similarity was one of the reasons she'd found Michael so comfortably easy to be around. It was just lately that the common ground between them struck her as potential quicksand. The nasty alluring draw she felt for Michael had developed into something far more complicated than "just friends." As deeply as she'd tried to bury those feelings, she was afraid he'd guess unless she were infinitely careful.

Michael glanced at her face as he turned into the driveway a few minutes later. "Listening to that old man, I couldn't help but wonder...in their time, do you think your Julia and my Benjamin heard the same legends about the ghost?"

"The thought crossed my mind, too," she admitted. "Although it's not like they needed any matchmaking ghost to get them into hot water. They managed that all by themselves."

"Did they? You haven't filled me in on the latest installment." He turned the key and doused the lights, parking right next to her car. "Have they made love yet?"

The question struck a nerve, but Simone didn't have to respond for a second. They both climbed out of his car, and she automatically started toward hers. Neither had planned on such a late night; she still had to drive home to her bed and breakfast. Michael reached her driver's door before she did, though, and then just casually leaned against it, as if waiting for her answer.

She'd had ample time, in the restaurant and on the drive there and back, to tell him about the latest developments with "their" lovers. Somehow she hadn't. Somehow, the way Michael's eyes rested intently on her face, she wished she could avoid the subject for another hundred years or so. "I finished reading the next two years, 1932 and 1933," she said swiftly. "All kinds of interesting things happened. King Kong came out. The Lindbergh baby was kidnapped. Prohibition was finally over, and almost fourteen million people were unemployed. James Hilton had a brand new bestseller called *Lost Horizon*—"

"And all that background is interesting, but somehow I'm still in suspense about the bottom line," Michael murmured. "Have they or haven't they made love yet?"

"It was an accident, Michael."

"Yeah?"

"They didn't mean to."

"No?"

"Julia came back to Maine, both those summers. She snuck away to meet him in this house, but all those times together, all those months...they hadn't *done* anything. She'd given up everything for her family. That was the way it had to be. They both knew there wasn't a prayer of a future. They'd both given up any hope of happiness in their private lives." Simone took a breath. "But there was this one night..."

"Tell me."

"Michael, they were so foolish, thinking they could keep it innocent forever. He was in love with her. I *know* he was. And she was crazy to be with him, lived for the few times they could be together—"

"Tell me," he repeated softly.

"They liked to dance, like I told you before. And sometimes, at night, they'd come out here to dance." Without meaning to, her gaze strayed to the shadows of the porch, where she'd already, too easily, imagined the lovers. "He'd set up a crank-up Victrola out here. And this one night, there was a crescent moon and a mist rolling in from the beach...."

"Like tonight?" Michael murmured.

"Like tonight. There was no one around, just the spoondrift and that misty fog swirling around them, and she wore that silly dress, the white one. And they were dancing to the songs of the day, 'April in Paris,' 'Night and Day'. But her favorite, the one she loved best, was 'Smoke Gets in Your Eyes,' and at first they were just dancing to that song, but somehow . . ." Her voice faded.

"That smoke-in-the-eyes song. How does it go?" Michael asked.

Simone turned her head. "Michael, you know how it goes. It's just one of those songs that's so old that everyone knows how it goes."

"I don't. Honestly. What are the words?"

She chuckled self-consciously. "I can't sing."

"You don't have to sing. Just tell me."

She said the words of the opening refrain. " 'They asked me how I knew/our true love was true/I of course replied/something here inside cannot be denied . . .' " Embarrassed, she chuckled again. "Well, I guess I can't remember all the words, either. There's another line about 'all who love are blind,' but the rest of that refrain is a blank. You get the idea, though. It's awfully schmaltzy and sentimental."

"Foolishly romantic," Michael murmured.

"Exactly."

"Can you sort of hum it for me? You said the words, and they sound vaguely familiar, but I still can't place the tune."

Because he asked, she hummed a few bars. It wasn't hard; the tune had been branded in her mind all day. She couldn't fathom why Michael suddenly moved toward her, though, couldn't imagine why he suddenly raised his hand.

She was carrying a purse. He shagged the strap from her shoulder, skimmed it down her arm and set the purse down with a little plop on the hood of the car. Then he lifted his hands again, this time both of them, in the classic gesture of a man asking a woman to dance. She thought he was joking. "Michael—"

"Keep humming it, okay? I'm just trying to imagine how it was with them."

He grinned and rolled his eyes, as if communicating that he already knew what a silly idea it was. The light of laughter in his gaze made her chuckle back, and then he took her in his arms and whirled her into the night. It felt crazy at first, plumb crazy to be waltzing in the dew-damp grass to no music but her off-key humming. Crazy... but fun. They swayed and dipped and whirled around the yard, until she suddenly couldn't catch her breath. His smile slowly faded. Her heart started spinning, not fast, but real, real slow, to the rhythm of that hopelessly romantic song about love that couldn't be denied. The spoondrift coming off the ocean shone like diamonds in the darkness, and fingers of fog swirled around them, and Michael... Michael was leading her deeper into the shadows, pulling her as close as his heartbeat.

Simone thought fiercely that she knew the difference between fantasy and reality. He wasn't Benjamin. She wasn't Julia. It was just that her heart had been so captured by the lovers' story. Her grandmother had made it so easy to imagine the feeling between the lovers in that long-ago time. Michael was so positive he had nothing in common with his grandfather. But Ben had given up on love, just the way Michael had. Maybe Ben would never have found love, any love, if Julia hadn't thrown caution to the wind

and reached out to him. They'd both been reckless.
They'd both been scared and scarred, but Julia had
never felt safe with another man. She'd never felt free.
With one man, only one man, she felt natural and
right, as if a secret, soft corner of the world could be
hers when she was with him. . . .

"Simone?"

She lifted her head. This was no fantasy. She knew
whose arms held her, saw, clearly, the man who'd given
up on love, who'd warned her that he only wanted
friendship. But the way Michael looked at her had
nothing to do with friendship. He'd looked at her that
way when he found her in the attic, as if she were a
stolen jewel, nothing that belonged to him, nothing he
had any right to touch. But that didn't stop him from
wanting to.

They were still swaying, half dancing, until he
ducked his head and kissed her. The hum died in her
throat. The first touch of his mouth was as soft as the
petal on a rose, a gentle brush, more tender than a
whisper. He tasted like ale and moonlight.

He kissed her again, luring kisses that asked, not
took, and then pulled her tighter into the nest of his
arms. Thick, rich kisses landed on her jaw, her throat,
making her light-headed, making her blood rush. His
hands stroked her shoulders, wound down the length
of her spine.

One kiss spun into another, wove into another. She
tried to warn herself that he didn't really need her. She
was imagining the drenched softness of those kisses,
imagining the stark, dark emotion in his eyes. It was
want-to-believe. She'd wanted-to-believe before with
men. She'd always been wrong.

Yet her arms tangled around his neck. Her whole body had turned liquid, and she had to have something to hold on to. Her fingers got lost somewhere in his thick sandy hair, clutched, when her body brushed against the cradle of his thighs.

He wasn't through dancing. She saw his smile when he lifted his head, a man's smile. He spun her away, pulled her back, waltzing her through the thick wet grass all the way to the shadowed porch steps. By the time he stopped, her heart was pounding and there was a roaring in her ears and his hands were on her blouse. Buttons popped. Slow. One at a time. The silky white fabric shivered down her shoulders, down and off her wrists, dropped somewhere in the shadows, and then he unhooked her bra.

Cool air whiskered over her skin. Her breasts were bared for his eyes. He found her breathtakingly beautiful, if she could believe the expression on his face. Breathtaking...but too short. He lifted her up a porch step, where it didn't matter a whit if she was too short for him, because all he had to do was bend his head to reach her. His lips lapped a tender path, a liquid path, between her breasts. Her spine arched when his mouth closed on one small, tight tip. He hurt her. A dulcet, delicious hurt that awakened every feminine nerve she'd ever had.

Although he caressed her breasts with treasuring slowness, she could feel urgency building in the tense, bunched muscles in his arms and shoulders. She told herself that men had wanted her before, that she knew precisely what passion was, but it wasn't true. Her roaring heart knew it wasn't true. Joy. That was the craziest part. She never remembered feeling this burst of joyfulness, this sweeping feeling of freedom and

wildness that made her feel beautiful, when she wasn't.
That made her feel infinitely wanted and desperately
needed and as if she were the only woman who had ever
existed for him, when none of that was remotely true.

He called her name on the sigh of a husky breath. So
silly, when she was right there, and certainly going nowhere when her knees were weaker than noodles and
she could barely catch her breath. He walked her up the
rest of the porch steps, and with an arm still around
her, reached for the front doorknob.

He never opened the door. If he meant to take her
inside, he seemed to forget the door, forget that in-
tent. It was smoky dark under the porch roof. He swept
her close again, so close she could feel his pulsing
arousal ironed against her, making shivers of heat pool
low in her stomach. He took her mouth again, his
hands threading in her hair to hold her still. He tasted
like a man who was claiming a woman he was dying
for, like maybe he would die if he couldn't have her,
who'd finally found someone he wouldn't, couldn't, let
go of.

She understood, in the yearning spin of an instant,
that they were going to make love unless she stopped it.
He'd never force her, she knew. He'd stop if she asked
him. She knew that, too.

But when she said his name, her voice was a clear,
soft calling for her lover, as if she were lost and had
been lost forever, and she was asking Michael to find
her. Her whole life she'd been sure, scared sure, there
wasn't an ounce of romance in her soul. But with him,
this was right. Even if this was a spell of love, momen-
tary, an illusion that could never last, with Michael, it
was right. It had to be. He loosened the button on her
pants. She pushed at the buttons on his shirt, pulled the

fabric loose and free, fumbled with his belt. Something made him smile. She saw his smile because she never looked at his body as she was peeling off his clothes; he never looked at her body as he was peeling off hers. They were looking in each other's eyes, like a magnet pull too compelling and powerful to break away from, too powerful to deny.

"Simone," he whispered, "I'm not Benjamin."

"I know."

"You're not Julia."

"I know."

"This is about us. No one else."

She heard him. His voice was like liquid gold, a caress in the rich deep silence of the night, his eyes on her skin another shivery caress. There had to be a million, zillion beds in the house, all of them more comfortable than a makeshift mattress of their clothes. The foggy mist was cool, damp, raising goose flesh on her breasts. None of it mattered. Nothing mattered but him.

He kissed her, warmed her, even as he pulled her down. Satin kisses fell on her face, her neck, matching the silk-satin kisses she poured on him. Length to length, both of them bare, she stroked him as ardently and wildly as he stroked her. His touch, his taste, told tales of loneliness and wonder. He hadn't known this would happen. He hadn't known he could feel this way.

Neither had she. Instinctively she wrapped her legs tight around his waist, pulling him to her, wanting him inside her. Now. Not later. Now, while this feeling was so huge and rich and joyfully loving, and if it were just a love spell, she didn't care. Nothing had ever been this right. No man had ever made her feel this way, and Michael . . .

He pressed in, gently at first, not hurrying, and her body seemed to melt around him, opening for him, drawing him in. His eyes were full of moonshine, silvery, dark and luminous, lanced her face as they molded together. He started a rhythm, the ancient rhythm of a love song that gradually increased in beat and tempo, carrying her on a current of desire so intense that she felt a raging hurt from the force of it.

She closed her eyes, her senses exploding, spiraling on his touch, his scent, the need she could feel firing through him. She told herself she was crazy to believe in magic, but that's what she felt, as if Michael were the magic and she was his web, taking him into her body as well as her heart. Yielding wasn't a choice. It was what she wanted to do for him, what she felt, as undeniable as air or water. She had the dangerous, terrifying sensation that she could fall off the world if he let her go.

He didn't let her go. Right when she fell, right when a thousand cataclysmic sensations rushed through her and peaked, Michael enveloped her totally in the safety and strength of his arms.

Eight

___

Any minute now, his heart was going to stop pounding. Any minute now, he was going to recover his common sense and move Simone inside before they both froze to death.

Not quite yet, though. For the first time in a decade, Michael was in no driving hurry to do anything. The porch floor was harder and colder than bricks—hardly a comfortable mattress—but he'd managed to pull her on top of him before they both collapsed. Her skin was damp, her silky fine hair all tangled, and her heart was still galloping as fast as his own. He had her anchored securely. Her cheek was nuzzled in the curve of his neck, her breath tickling him, and she hadn't stirred yet. Temporarily she was one whipped puppy.

So was he, yet wonder still simmered in his pulse. Wonder wasn't an emotion he associated with lovemaking... or with a woman. Sex was the best of biology, but it wasn't eye-opening, wondrous, earth-shattering. It wasn't holy spit stupendous.

At least, for Michael, it had never been before.

He never expected that dancing would lead to making love. His mind speared back to the moment when he'd pulled her into his arms and waltzed her across the lawn in the dark. Some men could pull off a romantic gesture. Not him. The impulse had been insane, foolish and potentially humiliating. There was no music; he couldn't dance, and Carla could have told her—his ex-wife would have *loved* to tell Simone—that he was a bungler anywhere near the romantic-gesture department.

Michael never liked failing. His masculine instincts were as honed and sharp as a fencer's sword for avoiding any circumstance where he was likely to fall flat on his keester. It was Simone's fault he'd forgotten that. When she started talking about "their" lovers, she'd gotten this look on her face. Her eyes softened, darkened. Her voice got this velvet tone. Somehow he'd gotten the feeling that she was dreaming about camellias and white dresses and the kind of guy who'd sweep her away.

Even when he coaxed her into his arms, Michael thought she'd laugh, think the whole idea of dancing was hoaxy. She hadn't. He was positive she'd pull back when he started kissing her.

But, oh God, she hadn't. He'd never had a lover ignite for him like that. He'd never had a woman... explode...cleaving to him as if there was only one mate in the universe for her, and it was him. She'd melted and he'd melted right with her. She was *his,* in a way no woman had ever been his.

Michael still didn't understand what happened to her. Hell, he didn't know what happened to him, either. But one thing was sure. Until he figured it all out, there was no way in this life that he was letting her go.

She shifted in his arms. Immediately his palm stroked down her back. The fog was rolling in as thick as a blanket, the air cool and damp. She'd been warm before, layered against the heat of his body, but her skin was chilling fast now. He needed to get her under cover.

"Michael?"

"Hmm?" He had to smile. Her voice was as sweet and thick as slow-pouring molasses.

"We didn't do so well at keeping that attraction under control."

"I noticed," he murmured. Gently he lifted her to a sitting position and possessively checked for damages. Even in the charcoal shadows, he could see a mark on the swell of one breast, her swollen mouth, her satin skin and her hair, Lord, her hair was really a mess. Smiling again, he pulled her to her feet.

"Thankfully we both know it was just sex, though, right? I mean ... it's understandable. We've both been alone a long time. Neither of us has to pretend it was anything more than that."

"I'm not much on pretending," he agreed.

"We're both only going to be in Maine for a short time. We'd really be nuts to make anything serious out of this. I'm sure you feel the same way...."

She was still talking as he unlocked the front door, gathered up their clothes, turned on a light and propelled her inside. The sudden artificial light made her wince. More to the point, he had a clear view of her face. His wildly abandoned lover, no question, was doing her best to metamorphose back into her pragmatic realist mode again. Michael didn't claim to understand her. He'd never again take for granted any assumptions about a woman's feelings. But he'd have to be deaf, dumb and blind not to notice the fragility and vulnerability in her eyes. The pulse in her throat was ticking like a nervous clock.

"I should go home," she said swiftly.

She wasn't going anywhere, but Michael sensed she'd balk if he put it just that way. "I was hoping you might sleep here. I have insomnia. Chronic, really bad. It would help a lot if you stayed."

"Oh." She appeared to think that over. "That's different, then. I didn't know about your insomnia."

Since she bought into that excuse, he elaborated at length on his pitiful long history with sleeplessness. For a few minutes, it seemed to distract her. He dropped their clothes on a chair, locked the door, and switched off the downstairs lights, holding her hand the whole time. He was still holding her hand as he led her upstairs. Her palm was a fair barometer of her emotions. It had been warm, now it was fast becoming damp with nerves, her fingertips less than steady, and she was looking just about everywhere but his eyes.

"Michael . . . I really don't know how this happened. You're probably feeling as upset and unsettled as I am."

"Actually I'm feeling angry."

"Angry?"

"Angry with myself. Not you. I've never in my life played Russian roulette with a woman. Hell, I had protection in my shaving-kit case. Not because I expected anything to happen—I honestly didn't, Simone—but it was just how our dad raised his sons. The rule was ingrained that a single man be prepared. As he used to put it, he didn't give a holy petoot how sure we were that nothing was going to happen. There are no excuses for a man failing to protect a woman."

She swallowed quickly. "I've never been irresponsible before, either. Ever. Not once. But it's the safest time in the month that it could be. And we were both carried away, Michael. It's my fault as much as yours."

"Not in my book. And maybe you'll worry less if it's a safe time, but I never bet in Vegas. If you're pregnant, you tell me. It would be our problem, not just yours. Okay?"

"Okay."

He waited while she slipped into the bathroom and closed the door. He heard the water running, imagined her using his peppermint-striped toothpaste, his brush, his towel and wondered what she'd look like with a baby in her tummy. His baby. From the look on her face when she came back out, the thought had crossed her mind, too. He suspected the idea of an unplanned pregnancy scared her—hell, how could it not?—but her eyes searched his with soft, luminous intensity. No woman had ever looked at him that way, not even Carla back in the days when they'd been in lust, in love, and blindly young.

He took her hand again. Simone could walk into the bedroom by herself. He just saw no logical purpose in taking the chance on her bolting.

Belatedly it seemed to occur to her that they'd been walking around stark naked. "I used to be thinner. I've gotten a little out of shape this summer—"

"You look in perfect shape to me." He said it matter-of-factly. He knew how uneasy she got about compliments. Still pulling her behind him, he detoured to

put his shaving-kit case by the bedside table, closed the
drapes on the French doors and folded down the quilt.

"My fanny's too chunky."

"Your fanny couldn't be sexier in a thousand years."

"My thighs... pounds just jump to my thighs."

"They're perfect, too."

"Michael... I'm a little nervous."

"I never guessed," he assured her.

"I just... never thought this would happen. Our
being together, our making love. I know you never
wanted to be involved. I don't want you to think this
has to change anything. We're both adults, after all,
and neither one of us is in the least a romantic ideal-
ist—"

"I know we're not," he murmured. And then, because he couldn't wait any longer, he kissed her.

By the time he lifted his head and ended that kiss, she
was lying beneath him on the downy feather mattress
and a freight train of emotion was running through his
head. Vaguely he wondered if she was always going to
bewilder him this way. He'd heard her nerves, the sensible caution in her voice, her labeling their making
love as attraction and "just sex." She'd always pro-
fessed to be a practical realist, and he didn't doubt her
sincerity. Simone had been honest with him from the
beginning, and for all he knew, that hour on the porch
had been a lightning-strike fantasy, a brief stretch of
insanity that could never conceivably happen again.

Only it *was* happening again. His antiromantic,
hardheaded, hard-hearted cynic melted against him
just like a rose opening for the sun. She called his name
on the cry of a whisper, sizzled his blood with her
treasuring kisses. He damn near forgot protection
again, and this time it was right there and handy. Sure,

he knew desire, but nothing like the head-spinning, soul-stroking, compelling power she inspired in him, with him, for him.

When it was over, she collapsed in his arms with a sleepy, feminine sigh. Within seconds, she was snoozing. Her head cut off circulation to his shoulder and her elbow jabbed right in his ribs, but he didn't move her. Wide-eyed in the darkness, he cuddled her close and stroked her soft skin.

Dammit, he was in love with her. Not only was that disastrous state of affairs never supposed to happen, but she was positively the last woman he should risk caring about. If he'd never understood Carla, he for sure would never comprehend Simone. Listening to her—*believing* her—had gotten him nowhere. Maybe that was some key factor to understanding a woman? Act on what she showed him, and pay absolutely no attention to anything she said?

He stared blankly at the dust motes on the ceiling, his heart thundering with agitation and his mind spinning a hundred miles an hour. He had no idea what she felt for him. None. What she called "just sex" was the closest to heaven he'd been to. She looked at him with love and denied in the same breath that she wanted any kind of involvement. And what she seemed to want— need—was a reincarnation of Benjamin. Not the scoundrel part, but old Ben had an undeniable gift for romancing a woman and making her feel cherished, beautiful, special. Michael just didn't know how to do that.

He thought he'd experienced every taste, texture and nuance of failure after Carla. Yet the fear of failing Simone hit him like a leaden weight in his chest. She made him feel differently, about life, about himself as a man. He'd break a leg before hurting her, but how could he possibly even dream of understanding her?

His thought train was interrupted by a husky sweet voice, murmuring right next to his ear. "Michael, close your eyes. You're going to sleep now."

His smile was automatic. Simone, of course, knew nothing about real insomnia. There wasn't a prayer on the planet that could make him sleep tonight. But because he didn't want to disturb her with his restlessness, he closed his eyes and lay still for just a few minutes.

Simone slowly unroped herself from Michael's arms and inched out of bed. There was no logical reason for such caution. A bomb wasn't likely to wake Michael; he was sleeping like the dead. Still, she tiptoed across the room and never turned on a light until she was behind the closed door of the bathroom.

The sudden glare of light made her blink. It took a moment before her eyes adjusted to the harsh brightness. The diamond-pattern tiles were frigid beneath her bare feet. She flipped the faucet on the pedestal sink and waited for the water to turn warm. The whole bathroom was designed for another age, with a bidet, an old-fashioned chain pull on the john and an ancient, free-standing bathtub with claw feet. The room had character and charm, but there was an odd, chilly draft coming from nowhere that made her shiver.

She dunked a washcloth into the hot water, started washing and abruptly stopped. She thought she caught a moving shadow in the mirror, but that was imagination— There was nothing in the reflection but her own face. That reflection was startling enough. The soft hint of a smile on her mouth . . . she hadn't known she was smiling. The green eyes staring back at her looked love struck, luminous, sleepy...nothing like her own. Her throat was rouged from Michael's whiskers; the crest of one breast had a telling mark; and the damn fool in the mirror was humming "Smoke Gets in Your Eyes"...at least until she realized it, and stopped.

She felt wonderful. The thought—the emotion—was damn near paralyzing.

The eerie draft whispered over her skin, as intimate as the caress of a hand, raising goose bumps. Obviously there was no one in the bathroom with her, but years ago her grandmother could well have stood right here, washing up after a night with her Benjamin, wearing the marks of her lover just as Simone had.

Julia had green eyes, too. The same oval face, and once, the same flyaway fine blond hair. Erase sixty years, and it could just as well have been Julia in that mirror. Simone hadn't read the last of the diaries yet. She truly didn't want to read any further. As much as she'd gained a new perspective and understanding of her grandmother, how could the lovers' story possibly end but in heartbreak? The bottom line was unavoidable. Julia had fallen for a forbidden man, a man she couldn't have; she'd invested her heart and soul in a love that had no future.

Simone pressed the washcloth tightly to her eyes. Had she forgotten all her common sense last night? Michael wasn't looking for commitment. He was lonely, and his turkey of an ex-wife had made him feel like a failure, and she happened to be there when he needed someone. They shared a common background, creating a closeness that had taken them both by surprise. But she'd be crazy—she'd be setting herself up for heartbreak—to imagine his feelings for her went deeper than that. Michael was just as forbidden for her as Benjamin had been for Julia.

Dread thrummed through her pulse. She wasn't falling in love with him. She'd already fallen, deep, hard and stupidly—and long before last night, if she were being honest with herself. Making love with him had intensified her feelings, though, and her heart clenched on a fist of fear.

Her cheeks still burned at some of the intimacies they'd shared in the night. She'd never lost her head before, never responded to any man the way she had to Michael. She tried to reassure herself that he couldn't know that. She morosely suspected that possibly—probably—every woman he'd made love with had responded as wildly and volatilely as she had. Michael was no ordinary lover. He couldn't possibly know how much last night had meant to her—not if she hid her feelings.

She'd always been outstanding at hiding her feelings. She'd always been tough, and practical, and downright cynical about anything to do with matters of the heart. She'd been terrifically repressed before, and damnation, she could become terrifically repressed again.

A quiet rapping on the door nearly made her jump out of her skin. She opened the door, and there was her matter-of-the-heart standing there, his sandy hair tousled, his body stark naked, his blue eyes still sludgy soft with sleep.

"You were gone," he accused her.

"Michael, I just had to go to the bathroom."

"You were gone a long time. I couldn't sleep without you." His voice was husky and luringly male. "What's wrong, honey?"

"Nothing." Yet he wrapped her in his arms as if he thought something was. His cheek nuzzled hers, less a kiss than just a physical connection. He yawned, smiling groggily at her.

"It's five-thirty in the morning. But you're wide-awake, aren't you?"

"I'm afraid so."

"Well, hell. There are only so many things you can do at five-thirty in the morning. In fact, I can only think of one."

Her eyes softened, luminous and vulnerable. Painfully vulnerable. She knew he meant making love.

"You want to?" he murmured.

Her stupid pulse didn't realize how tough she was. Her silly heartbeat was singing reckless, not repressed. She touched his cheek. "What'd you have in mind?"

"Crabbing."

"Pardon?"

"Crabbing," he repeated, and grinned at her.

The bait shop was open before daybreak. They'd catered to naive tourists before. The downhome Mainers were long on advice. "Ayuh, you have to have this," and "Ayuh, you have to have that." By the time they headed out, the once-pristine-clean trunk of Michael's New Yorker was jammed with wire traps, a bucket of chicken necks, and a rented black iron pot—the de rigueur method of boiling crabs, assuming they caught any.

"I hope you know what you're doing, buttercup, because I sure don't," he admitted to Simone.

"We'll be fine. I've done it before."

He knew she had. She'd mentioned crabbing on summer vacations when she was a kid, which was how the idea had popped into his head.

It wasn't his original idea. His original thought, when she stepped stark naked out of the bathroom at five-thirty in the morning, was to make love with her until noon. Maybe until noon the next day. But something had shaken her up. Repercussions, second thoughts, regrets, consequences about their spending the night together? Her face had been stark white, her eyes huge. He didn't know what to say. Hell, he never seemed to know the right thing to say around a woman, and he was afraid of doing or saying anything to upset her. The crabbing idea had been off-the-wall, but damned if it wasn't working.

They stopped by her bed and breakfast so she could change clothes. She'd chosen jeans, a bulky sweatshirt, old tennies, and being covered up in that kind of baggy attire seemed to make her feel more secure. She looked like a teenager with her hair banded in a ponytail. The color was back in her face, the dancing sparkle back in her eyes. She felt safe with him again, he noted. There was, of course, nothing romantic about a messy, sexless activity like crabbing.

Or there shouldn't have been.

They brought all the crabbing gear back home. The bait shop people had a dozen suggestions for great crabbing locations, but Michael had never met a fisherman who told the truth yet. Simone agreed that the saucer-shaped cove just beyond the lighthouse was as good a spot as they could get.

Mist was still skimming on the water when they first started, the sky softer than pewter with hints of rainbow color. Following her orders—she was getting a big chuckle out of instructing him by then—he tied the chicken necks inside the wire traps, then lowered the traps by rope-cord to the ocean bottom.

"What do we do now?" he asked her.

"We wait."

"Wait?" He scrunched up his brows, making her laugh again.

"You want me to spell it? You don't even recognize that word, do you? It'll be a few hours, Michael. The crabs aren't gonna just walk in the traps the instant you put them down."

"I don't wait well," he warned her.

They shucked off their shoes, cuffed their jeans and beachcombed for treasures. She found a kingfisher feather. He found her shiny stones. The sun rose like a veil in the buttery sky; the light caught diamonds on the rocky shore. Gulls joined them, but there was no one else up so early. He had her to himself. He talked about his kids, about coaching the Little League, about the first time he'd run a washing machine and all his white oxford shirts had come out a blotched blue. She told him about growing up in a household of all girls, the bickering and the wars, the secrets and the giggling.

Out of nowhere she brought up Carla. "You can talk about her, you know. You've never said what she looked like, what she's like."

Michael didn't know what she wanted to hear. "She's a redhead, attractive, five ten." Simone nodded, encouraging him to go on. "We met in college. Her major was art history, but we got married before she finished her degree. She liked decorating, that kind of thing, house stuff, parties. She got into a lot of causes." He hesitated, but Simone nodded again. Apparently she wanted him to go on. "I'm not sure what you want to know."

"It's not that I want to *know* anything. I just…" She gestured with her hand. "Michael, she was part of your life for a long time. I don't want you to think you can't talk about her, and maybe it would help. I mean…you still must have feelings for her."

There was no question in her voice. She sounded, in fact, very sure that he was still carrying a torch for his ex-wife. "Simone?"

"What?"

"She *was* part of my life, and sure, I have feelings for her. We had some good years. I'd have slayed dragons for her when we were first in love, and damn, over the years I sure tried to. But that's just a bank of memories now. She may have lost the feeling first, but believe me, there's no desire or love left in what I feel for her any more."

"Michael, you don't have to say that."

He hadn't intended to touch her. Every masculine instinct had red-alerted him this morning that she wanted a moratorium on touch and sexual feelings. But he couldn't have her believing that his ex-wife was on his mind in the way she seemed to think. Softly he cuffed her nape and pulled her to him, layered her mouth under his and took, outright took, a kiss that made his position clear. There was only one woman on his mind. It was her.

When he got around to lifting his head, his pulse was rattling and his blood pressure soaring off the map. Still, he smiled. Her lips were wet, silky wet, her throat still arched from the pressure of his kiss, and her eyes…damn, if she was going to keep looking at him that way, he was going to be tempted to take her there and then. For sure, though, she'd quit thinking about his ex-wife.

"Crabs," she said shakily. "We need to go check on the crabs."

There were only three in the trap by ten, but by the time the midday sun beat down, they'd caught nine bluepoints and some kind of slimy sea urchin. They built a driftwood fire on the beach. Once the blaze was going, they carted the traps to the yard so they could wash down the muddy, yucky critters with a hose. After that came the awkward business of collapsing the sides of the traps—which was how the crabs got in, and how the cook was supposed to get them out—but the little monsters were hardly volunteering to be put into the pot of boiling water.

Carla really wasn't on his mind, but inevitably the thought struck Michael that his ex-wife would have had an attack of the screaming meemies at the whole process. Carla was into white carpets and weekly hair appointments. She didn't like to get her hands dirty, had always hated anything to do with messes.

Simone was as spattered with mud and debris as he was by the time they hunched over the fire with plates and cracking tools. She'd melted butter in a small pot on the stones at the fire edge. Dipped in butter, the white meat was succulent, sweet, rich, every morsel worth the battle and the mess.

The sun blazed by then, and a congregation of gulls had settled down to watch the silly humans' antics. Vibrant, vivid sails dipped and swayed near the shore. The water was stinging cold. All Michael really noticed was Simone. God, she was happy. She loved this. It wasn't something he had to intuit, nothing he had to guess. She was relaxed and easy, her eyes brimming with laughter. He wondered when was the last time she'd just let herself . . . play.

"It's sure a long way from starched-shirt-and-tiedom," she teased.

"A rare treat for me," he admitted.

"Michael . . . did you ever think about keeping the house?"

Beyond their perch on the rocks, past the lighthouse and tall stand of fragrant pines, they could both see the top story of the house. He looked at it, then at her face. "All my work is in Detroit," he said cautiously.

"I understand. I figured it was impossible. It's just that I can picture your boys here, spending summers on the ocean, maybe coming for holidays. I bet they'd love it. It's a wonderful place for kids growing up."

"You've fallen for the old monster, haven't you?"

"Me?" The denials came fast and furious. "I'll bet she eats money in upkeep. For sure, she's nothing I could afford. Old houses like that take constant repair. Keeping her would be ridiculously impractical."

"That's what I thought, too." Michael hesitated, then said carefully, "And of course, your whole life is set up in Colorado—work, friends, home. You wouldn't want to leave all that."

"Well, no . . . but it wouldn't be as hard for me. I mean, you can't very well relocate a die-cast plant here. I like retail and marketing, but managing the ski shop was accidental. It happened to work out but I never had a big life goal to sell skis. I could probably find a way to open some kind of shop anywhere."

Michael paused again, expecting to feel an instinctive nip of masculine anxiety. He always felt nervous near murky waters, and God knew, the murky feminine waters of her mind were a total mystery to him.

Still, that leap of anxiety never happened this time. He heard what she said. But he also saw the way her gaze lingered on the widow's walk backdropped by the blue-pearled sky.

She was in love with the place.

"The more I look at her, the more I realize how impossible she'd be to keep," Simone said firmly. "Even for a vacation home, she'd be totally impractical. A money guzzler. She'd eat up your spare time in work. The only sensible choice is to sell her."

"I've always been practical," he agreed. "Like you."

"It'd just be nuts to take her on."

"Totally bonkers nuts," he concurred.

She cocked her head. "Do you realize how often this happens? We really think alike on an amazing number of things, don't you think?"

"We sure do." He curled his finger at her. "Come here, Simone."

Nine

Come here, Simone. Come here, Simone. Every time he'd used that particular phrase over the last week, Simone thought mournfully, she landed in trouble. There was something in Michael's voice that plugged directly into her electrical system and short-circuited her best efforts to be repressed and cool around him.

"Come here, Simone! It's ready!" Michael called out.

Simone winced. Did he have to use that phrase again? As predictable as sunshine, butterflies of anticipation soared straight to her pulse. Pure foolishness. Tonight she knew there was absolutely—positively—no chance of anything happening between them.

"Coming!" she called back. Juggling a mounded bowl of popcorn, napkins and pop, she headed for the parlor. Michael spotted her from the doorway.

His gaze dawdled from her baggy navy sweats to her bare feet. She should have expected his lazy grin.

"You took forever," he accused her.

"I thought it would take you longer to set this up." She set the snacks down on the coffee table, with a glance at the rented VCR. He'd not only hooked it up, but the movie was plugged into the slot and his hand ready on the remote control. "Are you really sure you want to see this? I don't want you to feel stuck for two hours, watching something you have no interest in."

Michael flicked off the lamp, leaving the parlor in dusty darkness. A tufty breeze pulled at the curtains, letting in sipping drafts of cool night air. He flopped on the couch, propped up his bare feet, and patted the cushion next to him. "It's not a matter of *wanting* to see this. It's a matter of research. I thought we both agreed? We have a better chance of understanding how Julia and Benjamin felt—why they made the choices they did—if we directly experience some of the things they went through."

"We did agree," Simone concurred. She could hardly fault that line of logical reasoning. Michael had, after all, the same motivation for wanting to understand his grandfather as she did her grandmother. From the beginning she'd willingly shared the information in Julia's diaries with him for the same reason. It was just that in the past week, Michael had taken their mutual family research into new and unexpectedly personal dimensions.

As she sank into the couch cushion next to him, Michael punched the button on the remote. The rented VCR promptly clicked on, and a fuzzy, silvery light flashed on the TV screen. The film was old, but not so old that she couldn't make out a romantic shot of San

Francisco's Golden Gate Bridge. And then, there he was. Gable. A young, sexy, unforgettably male and adorable Gable.

Julia and Benjamin had seen Gable in *San Francisco* in 1936, which was why Michael had gone to the extraordinary trouble of renting the VCR and finding the ancient movie. For her. For them. So they could try to understand what had motivated and moved their respective grandparents. Simone was more than willing to watch the film. She was just...nervous.

Michael reached for the bowl of popcorn. When he leaned back, he scooted closer. Close enough to tuck an arm around her shoulder. "It's a little chipper in here," he said matter-of-factly. "I don't want you cold. Have some popcorn."

She had some popcorn, but the weight and warmth of Michael's arm was far more diverting than the movie. He'd showered right after dinner, tugged on nothing more formal than old jeans and a loose pullover, but his chest was toast warm and snuggling next to him evocatively familiar. He was relaxed now, but she knew exactly how fast his muscles could bunch in sexual tension, how quick the lazy look in his eyes could change to the dark fires of desire.

"The film quality's really grainy," Michael said matter-of-factly.

"Terrible," Simone agreed, but so far she hadn't paid a lick of attention to the film quality or the story's plot. Her mind was solely on Michael—and her grandmother's diaries.

She'd finished the sections between 1934 and 1936 now. Lots of things had been happening in the world. Hitler had become führer in Germany; Mao Tse-Tung had snatched the reins of the Chinese communists;

London got its first television service in the form of the
BBC. Studebakers had cost $840 and Flash Gordon
and Buck Rogers were the reigning heroes in the comic
books.

Michael had seemed interested in all those details,
but they weren't the ones he picked up on. In 1935, a
new dance was all the rage—the rumba—and Julia had
fallen in love with it. Instinctively Simone's eyes
squeezed shut. "Come on, Simone." She could still
hear Michael saying it, still picture that silly night when
she'd taught him the rumba. They'd dipped and
swayed—and laughed—through the parlor, down the
front hall, outside on the moon-dipped porch. They'd
ended up making love on the floor in the parlor, their
clothes scattered like leaves in the wind.

"Are you cold, honey? You want me to close the
window?"

"No, I'm fine," Simone assured him, but she wasn't
fine at all. Michael's tone was again sensibly prosaic,
nothing to cause the shiver chasing down her spine, but
her mind leapt back to another afternoon. Broad day-
light, so hot they were both wearing shorts, she'd had
no clue that anything was coming. Michael had shown
up in the attic with a tray of caviar and crackers and
champagne. Ben had introduced Julia to caviar and
champagne the same way—even on the exact same en-
amel tray. "Come on, Simone," Michael had said.
He'd never gotten around to tasting caviar, he told her,
wouldn't she like to? So they'd tasted that caviar, and
they'd sipped that champagne, and somehow they
ended up making languid, slow love on a bed of old
clothes in the dusty attic.

Each time, Simone mused, they hadn't been doing
anything but researching their mutual family history.

Avoiding trouble should have been finger-snap easy. They were both committed to not repeating the judgment mistakes their grandparents had made. The problem was that her mind wasn't on Julia when they'd been rumba-ing through the house—or whenever Michael kissed her.

Her mind was on him. Michael was controlled, pragmatic, logical. And the most vulnerable man she'd ever known. He responded so instinctively, with so much volatility, to a woman's affection and caring. Thankfully he couldn't know how deeply her heart was affected. Surely he never intended her to interpret his actions as romantic. Michael considered "romance" to be a sentimental hoax.

So did she.

"Unbelievably corny," he murmured dryly.

Simone focused on the screen. "Talk about mawkish," she promptly agreed. "I can't believe the movie audiences bought into such unrealistic plots back then."

"Outright silly," he concurred.

His fingers feathered through her hair. He probably didn't realize he was touching her, she thought. Tonight really was entirely different. This was nothing like those other times, simply because there was no possibility of either of them wading into emotionally deep waters, no chance of intimacy. She'd gotten her period, which she'd awkwardly told Michael two days ago. She'd had to. They'd been careful—except for that first time—and it would have been terribly unfair to let him continue worrying that she might be pregnant.

Confusing Simone was her own unsettling reaction to the blasted cramps. She should have felt relieved, not disappointed. Her conscience should have whipped up a serious frenzy of shame for being careless, and instead she'd been daydreaming about babies with Michael's hair and eyes and gentle smile. Michael, typically, had responded to the news with a soothing question about whether she felt all right. But the point was that he knew she wasn't pregnant now. He knew they couldn't make it tonight. So there was absolutely no reason to think he'd rented an insanely romantic movie like this with any ulterior motive.

His hand drifted to her neck, a fingertip tracing the loose edge of her baggy sweatshirt. Desire cavorted through her pulse, arousing restless memories of how well he knew her as a lover. Michael had an unexpectedly dangerous imagination in the middle of the night. That train of thought was entirely inappropriate, she thought crossly, and forced herself to concentrate on the movie.

On the screen, Gable was about to pounce on his heroine. The camera zoomed on the star's face. Gable had craggier features that she remembered, Simone considered analytically. His skin was a little rough. Nothing like Michael's. Still, she noticed the oddest similarities. Both men had the same sandy-brown hair, the same startling sexy eyes, the same damned sexy *maleness*.

Gable kissed his girl. A chaste kiss. Quick. No tongues. Nothing like the X-rated stuff that was allowed in movies today.

Michael's mouth nuzzled the shell of her hair. Slow. A kiss involving his soft, damp tongue, and mainlining X-rated ideas directly to her blood pressure. "Come here, Simone," he murmured. Before that particular phrase could register warning bells in her mind, he eased her onto his lap where she could stretch out.

Where she could easily, naturally, wind her arms around his waist. Where he could take her mouth. Completely.

Simone hadn't been paying any attention to the movie. But she thought—there'd been no doubt in her mind—that he had. "Michael..."

"Hmm?"

"You haven't forgotten...?" she asked delicately.

"That you're temporarily out of commission? No. I don't think Gable's gonna get around to a consummated love scene in that movie. Neither are we."

"Then?"

He lifted his head, and possessively surveyed her flushed cheeks and still-parted lips. "Nights like this are meant for teasing. Remember when you were a teenager, scared to go too far? Half the excitement was knowing you were doing something forbidden. I think that was part of the emotional pull that trapped Ben and Julia. They rode that line for a long time, thinking dancing and moonlit dinners were safe, thinking a few kisses were safe, only they ended up teasing each other until they were both out of their minds. Maybe they really didn't know? Nothing, absolutely nothing, is more exciting than wanting what you can't have."

His voice was low, a husky burr of a murmur before he took her mouth again. Her senses swam in a deep, dark pool of swirling emotions. Maybe he never meant to, but he'd plugged straight into her deepest fears, her darkest desires. Surely every woman had fantasies of a reckless, forbidden love. Surely every woman dreamed of a love so strong, passion so compelling, that she couldn't help herself. Surely every woman, once in her life, dreamed of being...wicked.

It was how she felt with Michael. Reckless. Wicked. Damningly aware that she was inexorably spinning in the same web of mistakes that her grandmother had. Julia had taken the heart risk of a love affair that had no future. Michael had never once led her to believe that he felt love, much less that he wanted any kind of commitment from her. Simone never had any illusions. A woman who kept dipping her hands into the fire was just begging to get burned.

But Lord, what she saw in his face took her breath. Michael *knew* her, in a way no man ever had. His mouth crushed hers, sipping slowly, drinking from the taste and texture of her soft lips, her tongue. His palm slid under her sweatshirt, molding over her ribs, thumbing open the catch of her bra. Her pulse ricocheted when he claimed her breast. He'd touched her before. His thumb had rubbed and teased her nipple before, igniting the same dark, wicked excitement, the same rush in her blood. But it was different tonight, knowing she couldn't have him. It made her feel young and wild and innocent, as if he were her first love, her only love.

Silvery images flashed on the TV screen. The rest of the room blurred with ghostly shadows, yet she could clearly see his face, tautening with tension, his eyes darkening with fire. He was a grown man. Decades had passed since he was a boy who enjoyed being teased, who had the patience to start something he couldn' finish, yet there was a devil fire in his eyes.

"You like this, don't you, love?" he murmured. "Not to worry. I'll tease you good."

"Michael—"

"How far do you think we can go before we both burn up?"

"Michael—"

"Shh." With another kiss, he pressed her down into the couch cushions. Her mouth ached and her heart started slamming. There was a time she violently believed that she'd never understand her grandmother's immoral behavior. Now she did. His touch, his scent, his taste invoked a feeling of longing and belonging that she couldn't explain...or deny. It was never as simple as lust. There'd been no blaze in his eyes when she met him. Her so-contained, so-serious Michael had a mountain of emotion to express, to give, to share. To watch him coming alive had capsulized her own feelings.

Unbidden emotions bubbled to the surface. *Michael, I'm so in love with you that I'm scared to death.* That thought, never said, spilled into another. *I don't care if this is right or wrong. I don't care what the consequences are. No matter what happens, I'll never regret loving you....*

The entire morning had been an exercise in chaos. It was noon now, and Michael was slowly starting to unravel at the seams. Impatiently he clapped the telephone receiver against his ear. The phone call with Paula Stanford had wasted ten minutes already. "Paula, I promise that nothing wrong is going to happen in this house again. You bring on the customers. I'll have the place ready. No, no..."

He scraped a hand through his hair, pacing the length of the phone cord, then pacing back. Normally he thrived on problems and challenges, but this day he just couldn't seem to climb off the merry-go-round.

He'd spent two hours on the phone this morning with his purchasing and engineering people, and an-

other hour on the phone with his sons. Donnie and
Davie reminded him that he'd promised them a visit to
Maine if his trip took longer than three weeks—how
could he renege on a promise to his sons?—so that
flight had to be arranged. The landscaping crew was
due any minute. So was a moving van. Seth and Samantha wanted some of the antiques in the house
shipped to Atlanta—which Seth could easily have taken
care of when he was here, except that the lovebirds had
been so wrapped up in each other that they simply
hadn't. Michael volunteered to handle it. Hell, he could
handle all those kinds of challenges blindfolded.

None of that was the problem preying on his mind.

Momentarily Ms. Stanford paused for breath and let
him get a word in. "Paula, I told you, nothing funny's going on here. It's just an old house. Old houses
make noises. I've had an electrician and plumber out,
which I told you...."

Michael sank into the desk chair and closed his eyes.
Ms. Stanford was a pain in the keester. She wasn't,
though, the source of his unraveling nerves. Paula just
wanted reassurances that the house she was trying to
market wasn't going to fall down around her ears if she
dared bring out another customer. Ms. Stanford didn't
appreciate being embarrassed. "Lar, lad. She's up
there in the attic by herself, she is, and ye're down here
jabbering with another woman. Have ye lost yer
blooming mind?"

Michael pinched the bridge of his nose. Ms. Stanford didn't know what embarrassment was. Being ha-
rassed by a ghost that didn't exist—now *that* was
embarrassment.

"I have to tell you, lad, it's been a mighty relief to
see you cavorting all over the house with her. I had my

doubts when I first laid eyes on ye. Ye just looked a bit stuffy, ye know, like one of them stiff aristocrat types. I was prepared to coach ye, of course, considering the limitless experience I've had seducing women. Instead, ye've taught me a thing or two. Whew. What ye two managed on the kitchen table last night defied anything I ever saw...."

Paula was still on the telephone. Tentatively, very tentatively, she was attempting to set up a date and time to bring a customer out. Michael missed the whole exchange. He grabbed for a paper and pencil. "Just a minute. Say that again?"

"Quit talking to that blowsy woman, lad, and listen to me. What I dona understand, what I canna fathom, is what ye're waiting for. You have not told her what ye feel. It doesn't take a big mind to figure out that she'll leave ye, lad, she'll be gone faster than wind, if she doesn't know ye love her."

"Will you shut up?" Michael snapped, and then sucked in a breath. Soothingly, quietly, he said into the phone, "No, of course I wasn't talking to you, Paula. There were just some workers outside, making a lot of background noise, and I couldn't hear you. What was that time and day again?"

A few minutes later, he hung up the phone. By then, predictably, the ghost voice had disappeared. For a brief stretch, the whole house was quiet. Dust motes danced in the afternoon sun; a hummingbird hovered just outside the window. In the distance he could hear the rhythmic roll and splash of surf on the rocks.

Michael sat motionless. Jock's intrusions no longer unsettled him. Why bother worrying about Jock? He had ghosts of his own.

For days now, he'd wanted to tell Simone that he'd fallen in love with her. He hadn't. Fear paralyzed him every time he tried. Not the fear of rejection, but the deadweight fear that he'd misread her feelings completely.

For a man who'd never been good at reading a woman's mind, Simone was the ultimate risk of failure. Everything she told him was the opposite of what he knew. Or *thought* he knew. She'd deny to the death being a romantic— And she wasn't lying; she really believed that. But the truth he perceived was that she was a hopeless softie and a sentimental romantic to the core. She liked dancing and music and quiet evenings. She liked surprises. She liked sunsets and roses and poetry. Sometimes she liked slow hands, and sometimes . . . and sometimes she liked to be taken hard and fast, to feel swept away and seduced. Hell. Michael never planned to play out the history of the old lovers, and he sure as hell never anticipated finding anything to respect in his rascal of a grandfather. But Benjamin, damn him, had seemed to understand a woman's heart. And following up a few of old Ben's romantic ideas had somehow become a catalyst for his own.

Startling Michael was the painful self-discovery that romance was never his nemesis. Caviar every day—no. On an everyday basis, he was a suit-and-tie guy, just as Simone was tailored and practical and neat. But when the workday was done, he loved thinking up ways to surprise her. When he was with her, alone, he felt the increasing freedom to be someone else, to be the kind of man and lover that—once—he never thought he could be.

He'd been contained with Carla. He'd believed that was what she wanted from him—a man who was a decision maker, a source of security and control. If he'd been wrong, it struck Michael now that he'd been even more wrong about himself. Carla had no interest in his vulnerable side. She'd always cut him off when he talked about what he was thinking or feeling. Their marriage had been a locked box. He'd been as trapped in it as she. He didn't know that he could be . . . more. That there was more to feel in life, more to experience as a man and a lover, than he'd ever guessed.

Until Simone. Michael stared blankly at the stucco ceiling. She'd become his world, captured a niche in his heart more important to him than breathing. But he'd never accurately judged a woman's emotions in his life. To push Simone toward something she didn't want or need was to risk hurting her. How many times had she vociferously claimed that "just sex" was all she wanted? How many times had she violently denied having any trust in love or romantic feelings? Dammit, was he supposed to believe her . . . or what his historically ace bungler-of-a-heart told him?

It was Simone's fault—entirely—that he was slowly, unwillingly, beginning to trust his masculine instincts. But he needed time, Michael thought glumly. Time to convince her that he wasn't going to seduce and abandon her the way those other guys did. Time to prove that she could trust him. Time to indelibly show her that the feelings of love between them were real.

The nightmare problem was that he didn't have time. Weeks had already passed. His business was waiting and her vacation was nearly over. Unless something drastic happened over the next seven days, he was afraid he was going to lose her.

Simultaneously he heard the muffled clattering of shoes on the second floor and a pounding on the front door. He swung out of the desk chair.

"Michael? Where are you?"

"Right here. I'll get the door...you don't have to run."

At the same time he yanked open the front door, Simone was pelting down the stairs. The intruders were two skinny, shirtless kids from the lawn-care service. All they wanted was to announce they were there and ask if he had any special instructions. He gave them their blasted instructions, but his gaze riveted sharply on Simone.

She'd headed up to the attic two hours before in a fine mood. Something had happened. He had no idea what. Her white slacks had a crease and her emerald-green pullover was neatly tucked in, so there was no clue that she'd been in any messes. But her face was oddly pale; she was twisting her hands, and dammit, the nerves pooling in her soft green eyes were outright scaring him.

The instant the lawn-care boys were out of sight, she started talking. "Michael, I need some boxes. It looks like a heck of a mess up there, but it's finally all sorted out between trash and keepers, things I think you and your family might want, things I'd like to ship home—"

"You want boxes, I'll get you a hundred boxes, so just forget about them, okay? What's wrong?"

"Nothing. Everything's fine. I finished the last of the diaries, in fact," she said cheerfully.

The telephone rang. She tried to sprint past him to answer it. "No, just let the answering machine get it," he told her. Outside he heard the wheezing sound of a

diesel engine; it had to be the moving van pulling in—
yet another interruption. Was there no end to the noise
and confusion? Ignoring all of it, Michael propped a
foot on the stairs, determined to pin her down, for at
least a few minutes. "So," he said calmly, "what happened in the last diary?"

"Well…it was 1937. They saw *Gone With The Wind*
together. And they read Steinbeck's *Of Mice and Men*.
Milk was only ten cents a quart, can you believe that?
The new dance of the day was the jitterbug—"

Geesh. How she loved those details. "Simone,
maybe you could fill me in on the background later?
What *happened* between Benjamin and Julia?" He
sensed the diary was the cause of her stress, but getting a straight answer was like pulling teeth.

"Do you know Rupert Brooke? The poet?"

Hell, no. The only poet he knew was Shakespeare,
and that was only because Will had been force-fed to
him in high school. "Just tell me about it," he said
gently. Her eyes darted to the parlor window. The
lawn-mowing tractor was starting up, making a roaring racket. From the front yard came the distracting
sound of men's raised voices. "Forget all that. Forget
there's anyone here but you and me for a minute,
okay? What about this poet guy?"

"Julia put a line from Rupert Brooke in the diary. 'I
said I loved you once; it's not so. Such long swift tides
stir not a landlocked sea.'"

The metaphor was real pretty, but if it had some deep
meaning for Simone, it sure as hell escaped him.
"Okay. So…?" He prodded her.

"So she ended it, Michael. She was landlocked. That
was the bottom line. No matter how much she loved
your grandfather, she was married, and she was hold-

ing Benjamin back from finding anyone else as long as she allowed the relationship to continue."

Her soft green eyes met his. There were volumes of emotions in those eyes if, just once, he knew how to read them. "Honey, you knew the affair had to end at some point."

She nodded quickly. "Of course I did. And technically, I suppose you could say that it all worked out fine—for Julia. Loving Benjamin changed her. Loving him gave her courage and confidence. She was a different woman when she ended it, stronger—strong enough to stand up for herself. She never saw Benjamin again, but she went back and made a marriage. She never tolerated any more abuse; she and my grandfather eventually had a child, lived together for a lot of years. I'm not saying it's *right* that Julia was unfaithful, but how can I have the arrogance to judge her? Maybe none of that could have happened if she'd never met and loved Ben. But what about him?"

"What do you mean?"

"I mean…what about how the affair affected Ben? Do you know what happened to your grandfather after that?"

Michael frowned. "Well, I never had a diary of his life to go by, and I'm not real clear on dates, but he was married and divorced a couple of times. Believe me, there was never a shortage of women in his life—"

"Oh, Michael. That was exactly what I was afraid you'd say. Don't you see how terribly she hurt him?"

Actually he didn't, but just then the lawn mower chose to clatter right past the open window. The phone rang again. Someone started rapping insistently on the front door. Michael clawed a hand through his hair, his gaze still magnetized on her face. He was missing something. Dammit, he needed a course in bewildering women. He just couldn't shake the sick feeling in his gut that she was talking about more than how Julia had ended a love affair. She was talking about ending their own.

"I don't see that she hurt him," Michael said cautiously. "I mean...nothing that happened was her fault. It was a different time, a different era. Your grandmother was trapped in a marriage she couldn't get out of. Her being trapped affected her choices."

"And Ben's," Simone said softly. "I think he really loved her, Michael. Emotionally she moved on, but he didn't. He never made another relationship work, did he? She let the affair go on too long. She said she loved him, but ultimately she hurt him. It was a selfish love. It was just...romance. She was just *pretending* to be the woman in his life—"

The front door squeaked open. A man's voice yelled out, "Yoo-hoo!" The telephone jangled again and the bull-roar of the lawn mower was enough to make a sane man pull out his hair.

"Dammit," Michael snapped. He wagged a finger at Simone. "We're not through talking about this." The man at the door belonged to the moving van outside. He was built like a Sherman tank, with a full red beard and shoulders bulging with muscles. Wedged behind him were two lanky teenagers, the rest of his crew. They had to be shown which antiques to move, from where, and in the meantime Simone zipped down the stairs for the telephone.

There was just no way to put the chaos on hold. It'd be all right, Michael told himself. He'd talk to her later, when the house was quiet and he had her alone. He understood she'd always been afraid of turning out like

Julia, but nothing the older lovers did had anything to do with him and Simone. As soon as they caught some private time, he could surely make her see that.

Brusquely he handled the moving people and started directing traffic. The Sherman-tank redhead was just wheeling in a dolly cart when Simone hustled back from the phone. "I just talked with your sons," she announced.

"Yeah?"

"They sound adorable, Michael."

"Lots of people get that mistaken first impression," he said dryly. "Trust me, they're a pair of hellions in person."

"Apparently we're going to find out. You'll need to call your ex-wife back pretty quick. I'm not sure what travel arrangements you made for the kids, but the airlines just called Carla about the chance for seats on an earlier flight. They want to come on a flight arriving at midnight tonight."

Ten

The wooden swords clicked and slashed the length of the attic. The duel had been raging for some time. Sweat flowed freely. Screams of pain and fear echoed in the air. The pirate with the black eye patch leapt on a rickety chair. "I'm gonna slay you, you bloody pig-eating son of a platypus!"

"In your dreams, you yellow-bellied thief of a carnivore!"

Both pairs of blue eyes darted to Simone, checking to make sure she was duly impressed. Simone's hand leapt to her throat, expressing appropriate shock and horror. She waited a few more minutes before casually remarking, "You guys look pretty hot. When you're done with the killing spree, I've got some lemonade over here."

"Lemonade?"

"Lemonade?"

The wooden swords clattered to the floor, forgotten. Simone starting pouring. The pirates were well matched, with the same eye patches, the same inconquerable cowlicks, and the same dinosaur T-shirts. In the first days, Simone had trouble telling the twins apart, but no more. Both were physical clones of their father, but Donnie had Michael's energy and drive and take-charge determination. Davie was the spitting image of his dad, too, but in a different way. He was the imaginative one, the thinker who tended to hide his deeper feelings. Simone had fallen hook, line and sinker for both of them, an inevitable problem considering how much time they'd spent together.

Michael had taken the crew sailing, crabbing, swimming. They'd made a bonfire on the beach one night and roasted marshmallows, traipsed around the outdoor art fair in Bar Harbor another day and twice driven to Acadia for hikes and picnics. Simone had protested about being included, not wanting to intrude on Michael's private time with his sons, but he'd rolled his eyes as if that idea were ridiculous.

The first cup of lemonade spilled. "Yikes," Donnie said guiltily.

"No sweat." Simone had been around them a week. She'd brought up a fresh roll of paper towels for cleanups. She'd also carried up masking tape and address labels, but the process of packaging her grandmother's things had been inevitably slow going with all the help.

"Whatcha think Dad's doing?" Donnie asked.

"Cleaning up downstairs. Remember? Ms. Stanford is bringing customers this afternoon."

"Yeah, I remember," Davie said glumly. "I remember we're supposed to go home tomorrow morning, too. We don't want to go. And we don't think Dad should sell the house, either. Can't you talk to him, Simone?"

"Honey, his work and his business are all in Detroit. And so is your school and your mom."

"Schools are everywhere. What's the difference? And mom wouldn't care if we stayed here with Dad. She's really busy with George." Donnie's nose scrunched over the name George, who was apparently his mother's newest boyfriend. "And Dad's happy here. I've never seen him so happy. He's having fun and he isn't working all the time and everybody loves it here."

Her throat suddenly felt thick, as if a clog of oatmeal had lodged there. "I know, sweetie."

"You could marry him," Davie suggested. "Have you thought about that? If you married him, you could talk him into keeping the house and staying here."

"I think," Simone said gently, "that grown-ups need a stronger reason than that to get married."

"Well, sure. But you like my dad, don't you? And he likes you. And we like you. I mean, the whole thing's perfect, you know? What's this?" Donnie, whose hands were never still for long, picked up a heavy triangular prism.

Simone leapt for the diversion. "It's a seaman's prism. Made of green glass, I think. In the olden days, they didn't have electricity or lamps below deck. So the sailors wedged the prism in a place where it would catch and refract the light." She held it up, so they could see how the smallest ray of light exploded in all directions from the prism.

Most unwillingly, the memory of making love with Michael in the attic lanced through her mind. Neither had noticed the prism stashed on the windowsill then. It was later that Simone had. The light had jeweled colors on Michael's face, his bare chest, his hands moving over her body. The memory made the lump in her throat feel bigger than a boulder.

"Can we have the prism?" Davie asked.

"It's yours," Simone assured him. "It's one of the things I'm packing up in the boxes for your dad."

"It doesn't seem fair. You get all the girls' underwear and goofy stuff, and we get all the good things."

"It's okay. I like the girls' stuff."

"I guess you can't help it, huh? Being a girl and all yourself. You think the prism belonged to the ghost?"

"Yeah, you think it belonged to Jock?" Donnie echoed.

Thankfully the twins were enthralled with Jock's legend. Actually they were enthralled with anything that involved blood and guts and terror. While she continued packing, she kept them busy telling stories. Having the boys around had saved her life this past week, she thought gratefully.

Michael had tried to start a serious conversation with her a dozen times. He'd taken her in his arms more often than that. Naturally with the boys around, though, she'd gone back to sleeping at her bed and breakfast. And during the days, two nine-year-old urchins could be counted on to reliably interrupt any prayer of a private moment.

It was best. Her flight home to Colorado was three days from now. She knew Michael. He never left a problem hanging. Eventually they were doomed to one of those awful, awkward conversations when he ended the relationship, but later and quicker was infinitely better than painfully prolonged.

Being around the boys had put everything back in perspective. Michael's life was his sons and his work and a thousand other things that had nothing to do with her. A vacation interlude was nothing like real life. Heaven knew how she'd let herself forget that, but reading the last diary had been a slam-dose of reality. Champagne in the afternoon, dancing in the moonlight—that wasn't real. Like Julia, she'd been playing at romance. Like Julia, she'd been pretending that falling in love—that *love*—could make everything all right.

"Hey? Whatsa matter, Simone?"

"Nothing, sweetie."

"Did you hurt yourself?" Donnie sounded hopeful. The rascal was always willing to swap scraped-knee tales.

"I'm fine," she said, and schooled her expression into a light smile. But she wasn't fine. She had the terrible feeling that she was never going to be fine again. Her chest hurt with a sharp ache, as if something fragile deep inside her was splintering into shards.

She hadn't just fallen for Michael: she'd dropped straight off the cliff. They'd shared troubles and laughter, making love and brushing teeth together. She knew how personally he'd taken the failure of his divorce, how careful he was to avoid hurting a woman's feelings. She loved his sneaky sense of humor, the way he barged into problems headfirst, the look of his sleepy eyes when he first wakened in the morning. She more than loved him. She couldn't imagine her life without him.

Her conscience inexorably reminded her that she hadn't asked for this heartache. She'd all but begged for it. Hadn't Julia's story taught her anything? The

Hartman women were infamous for confusing romance and love. Michael had been painstakingly honest about not wanting to be seriously involved. She had no business expecting him to love her. She had no business expecting promises or commitments. She'd volunteered for the affair. He'd never forced her. She'd made out like she could handle it.

And she *could* handle it, Simone told herself firmly. That was the difference between herself and Julia and all the other Hartman women. She was practical and pragmatic and a hard-core realist. She was tough.

It was just, right now, she didn't know how to be tough enough to walk away from the only man she'd ever loved.

"Geezle beezle." Donnie squinted at her face. "Are you *crying*, Simone?"

"Heavens, no. I just got something in my eye."

"Like an eyewinker?"

"Like an eyewinker," she agreed.

"Hey." Davie piped up from the window. "Somebody's driving up."

"It's probably Ms. Stanford and the customers. We'll just stay up here and be quiet, okay?" Simone twisted around the boxes and debris to look below. "Oh, dear," she murmured.

"What?"

"What?" Davie echoed.

"I think there's a tiny possibility that your dad might need some help. I'm going downstairs, just in case. Will you guys be okay up here for a few minutes?"

"Sure."

Simone clipped down the stairs to the first floor, thinking that she was probably being foolish. Michael didn't need her. Michael was a Class A coper with any problem. Maybe her protective instincts had gone on red alert when she caught a look at the customers. Except around her, Michael could be strangely nervous around the female of the species—but this was hardly the same thing.

She reached the hall, in time to overhear Paula talking with Michael. Paula was wearing a typically frilly short dress, yet for once, her manner was almost subdued. "They're walking around the yard, but they'll come in any minute. I should probably have warned you, Michael. If you have any problem with the kind of people you're willing to sell to—"

"*Kind* of people? What's that supposed to mean? I don't care if they're Laurel and Hardy as long as their money is green."

"Oh, their money is green," Paula assured him. "And they have lots of it. It's just..."

"Just what?" Michael was pushing down the cuffs of his plaid shirt, looking confused by the whole exchange. Abruptly he turned his head and saw the two men heading up the porch steps. Simone came up behind him and clamped a hand in his, making it perfectly natural for her to be included in the introductions.

Mr. Latham was wearing a lavender silk shirt, white duck pants and open sandals. He was accompanied by Mr. Clairborn, in a pink silk shirt and shorts. Mr. Clairborn wore an earring and an ankle bracelet. Mr. Latham was wearing more gold around his neck than Simone ever dreamed of owning and liberally laced his conversation with "darlings." Both gentlemen were oohing and aahing before they reached the front door. Simone could have been mistaken—how could anyone tell someone's sexual persuasion solely from appearances?—but she definitely suspected that the boys were in love.

Conceivably the same thought had occurred to Michael. Not that his smile wasn't infinitely polite, but once introductions were over, conversation floundered as noticeably as a beached whale. "So," Michael said heartily, "your field is interior decorating?"

It seemed it was. They owned a successful firm in Portland and did a lot of traveling down the coast. They wanted a hideaway, a place where they could be alone.

"Alone," Michael repeated, his tone again hearty. He looked frantically at Simone.

"Maybe we should show them the house," she said smoothly.

There now, Simone thought, that little prod was all he needed from her. It was logical that the feminine nature of the gentlemen would throw him for a minute, but she'd seen Michael in action before. Whatever his personal feelings, he never let them show. Business was business, and as he walked the men around, Michael was typically well prepared with facts and figures about the property.

Truthfully, though, his inveterate honesty and integrity seemed to get in the way of his salesmanship today.

"The taxes, I have to admit, are a real bear. And probably going to get higher."

Mr. Clairborn frowned. "You have reason to think there's a property tax increase in the mill?"

"Well, it's a still growing tourist area. What can you expect?" Michael smiled disarmingly, and led them through the utility room, mentioning electric and water costs and then showing them the furnace. "She's a real beauty, isn't she? As old as she is, you won't have to worry about *her* running well.'' He hesitated. ''Although I have to be honest with you. She uses number two grade fuel. It costs an arm and a leg to keep a house this size warm in the winter, but you were probably prepared for that, weren't you?''

Mr. Clairborn tugged on his earring. ''Exactly how much do you mean by an arm and a leg?''

''Hey, nothing much more than a thousand a month. Especially if you shut off some of the rooms, and don't mind wearing a jacket. I have no problem living around fifty-five degrees. It just takes a little getting used to.''

''Fifty-five degrees?''

Simone shot a startled look at Michael. Her hand was still cuffed in his, the connection as inseverable as an umbilical cord, but she couldn't catch his eye. She supposed that, Michael being Michael, he felt he had to be honest about heating costs. But instead of pointing out the new face-lift in the kitchen, he regretfully mentioned the age of the appliances. And instead of playing up the charm and character of the Victorian fixtures, he studiously admitted the archaic plumbing.

Mr. Latham and Mr. Clairborn exchanged several meaningful glances, but still, Simone said nothing. Michael couldn't help being hopelessly honest, and the boys were only momentarily distracted by the house's flaws. They both fell hard for the architecture. Mr. Latham trilled a steady litany of ''fabulous'' and ''marvelous'' at the stained-glass window on the landing, the high-pitched ceilings, the window seats and cubbyhole alcoves.

Michael patiently listened to that litany—the whole tour was going smoothly, Simone thought—until he herded the group upstairs. The gentlemen had just stepped on the second-story landing when a galloping pounding resounded from the ceiling. "Good heavens, what's that?"

"Don't worry," Simone said. "It's just..." She started to tell Mr. Latham that it was just the children playing in the attic, when Michael interrupted her.

"Ah, hell," he said boyishly. "Should we tell them, honey?"

Simone stared at him blankly, but he was facing the other men.

"Simone thought we should keep quiet about the ghost, but hell, I told her, it's nothing to hide. Nobody's scared of a haunted house these days. The whole thing's kind of fun. It's not as if the ghost ever does anything *dangerous*."

"Michael," Simone snapped under her breath, "are you out of your mind?"

He squeezed her hand affectionately. "Okay, love. I get you. I won't say anything else... here's the master bedroom and there're two full bathrooms up here. Huge, isn't it? I'm afraid it's more set up for a family and children than just a couple of single guys—"

"Ghost?" Mr. Latham echoed.

"Jock's his name," Michael confided, and added reassuringly, "Nothing to worry about. Really, he's rarely any trouble during the day. Of course at night, I have to admit, some of his tricks can be a little aggravating when you're trying to sleep."

"You're putting us on, Mr. Connor."

"Make it Michael."

"Fine, then. Michael—" Mr. Clairborn's voice pitched to a soprano when a bed pillow hurled through the door of the blue bedroom. "My word— Who's in there?"

"No one. Don't you worry about a thing. Like Mr. Latham said, I was just putting you on." Michael smiled roguishly. "Real chestnut floors up here. Don't find many of those any more— Aw, hell."

"What's *that?*" The whole crew heard the sound of water gushing, as if someone had turned on the showers and faucets in both bathrooms full force.

Michael released her hand and took off at a jog toward the farthest bathroom. "Nothing," he sang out cheerfully. "Any house this old has its little personality quirks, you know? Jock, you behave yourself for our guests, you hear me?"

Thundering footsteps responded from the floor above. Pipes clattered and clanged. Somewhere, a window slammed. Simone never took her eyes from Michael's face. Boy Scouts should look so innocent. His eyebrows arched in befuddled surprise when Mr. Clairborn started swearing and grabbed his friend's arm.

"Hey, where are you guys going?"

The boys were halfway down the stairs when Paula stuck her forefinger in Michael's face. "I've had it! This is it! Our business relationship is severed as of this instant. You can eat your commission, for all I care, and I hope you rot in this monster of a house until doomsday and never sell it, do you hear me?"

Paula didn't wait around for an answer. She stalked down the stairs in a huff, slamming the front door on the way out hard enough to crack plaster. *"Geesh,"* Michael said, "what on earth got into her?"

"You *know* what got into her. And you're lucky she didn't kill you. I was tempted myself."

"Hey. I didn't throw the pillow in the hall. I didn't turn on all the faucets. It must have been Jock." Mi-

chael held up his hands in the classic gesture of innocence. "I think he doesn't want us to sell this house.
Wasn't that your first theory? That the ghost was sabotaging any effort to show off the place?"

Simone poked a finger at his chest. "*Don't* try to
confuse me, Michael. You were mean to those guys."

"Not deliberately. I had nothing against Laurel and
Hardy. To each their own. I just really didn't think this
house was right for them. Did you?"

"You're confusing me again," she accused him.

"What'd I say now?"

It wasn't what he said. It was what he was doing.
First his gaze darted right, then left, and then he moved
straight toward her. She retreated a step. He stalked
closer, real quiet, real slow. "Michael, you're making
me nervous—"

"Are we alone in this hall? Are we actually, finally
alone for the first time in this entire week?"

She didn't have the chance to answer. When her back
grazed against the wall, he pounced. His mouth pinned
hers with unerring aim. It was a lonesome, winsome
kiss. The hall was pearl gray with shadows, cool and
dim and absolutely quiet except for the sound of his
breathing. The only light was the masculine gleam in
his eyes, and he liked it just fine when she went limp in
his arms.

"You love this house, Simone," he murmured.

"You know I do. But—"

"And you fell in love with my hellion sons at first
sight, didn't you?"

"You know I did. But—"

Michael didn't seem to realize that they were old—
way too old—to neck against a wall, layered against
each other like teenagers. Nothing about his eyes re-

minded her of a boy's, though. And he knew what to
do with his hands that a teenager never dreamed of.
Still, he kept talking. "We had a great time this week.
Skinned knees and mosquito bites and constant inter-
ruptions. Kids' fights. Spilled milk. The phone ringing a hundred times an hour and no time to breathe,
much less talk, but I never saw one thing throw you for
six. You liked it all."

"Sure." What was not to love? She had no idea what
he was getting at.

Michael stopped playing, stopped smiling, and simply took her hands in his. Palm to palm. Fingers twined
between each other. "There's been no champagne and
caviar, Simone. And unlike that song—no smoke in
either of our eyes. You're not Julia. And I'm sure as
hell not Benjamin, although I tried my best."

"You were trying to be like your grandfather?"
There didn't seem to be a breath of air in the whole
hall. How many times had he told her that he never,
never, wanted to be like his grandfather?

"He seduced her. Couldn't you read between the
lines of all those diary entries? He plied her with all the
things she was vulnerable for. Personal time, someone
to listen, music and dancing, the caviar of attention,
the champagne of caring, romance. I've tried. I've
tried like to hell to be like him. Maybe it wasn't right.
You seemed to figure out that I was just playing at romance, but I've never known a woman I wanted as
much as you, and there was nothing I wouldn't have
tried to win you. But dammit, he lost her. Is that the
way this stupid story always has to end?"

Simone told herself not to jump to any wild conclu-
sions about what he meant. She told herself when a
woman's heart was beating louder than thunder, and a

man had been frustrated by deprivation for a week, and he hadn't been sleeping, and the look in his eyes was as deep as a river, she didn't have a prayer of thinking clearly. It was probably silly to even try. She touched his cheek softly. "Michael—"

"I don't care what they did wrong. I know what they did right. They took a chance. They took a risk. Maybe I don't know what you want. Maybe I'm terrible at reading you. Maybe I don't understand. I can't claim to understand. You've bewildered me from the day I met you, but I swear, Simone, I swear—"

The attic door swung open with a bang. Two sets of boys' hiking boots clattered through the doorway at racehorse speeds.

"Hi, Dad!"

"Hi, Dad!"

Eleven

The kids had flown out last night, and temporarily the house was as quiet as a cave. Michael was even gone. He'd left a half hour before on a quick trip to town, promising he would bring back take-out Chinese for dinner.

Simone was painfully aware they only had one evening left together. Her flight home left at three tomorrow. She'd scurried around all day packing up the last boxes in the attic, but that project was finished now—except for the one small case she'd deliberately left open.

A warm summer rain pelted the attic windows. Swords of lightning flashed in the darkening sky, and the sound of a moody, gloomy wind seeped through the cracks. It was crazy weather to be standing there stark naked. Simone shivered, although not from cold.

The lantern pooled a hazy circle of light on the open suitcase. Carefully Simone lifted out the red satin nightgown with the black lace trim. The satin was faded, the lace fragile with age, but the flaws were barely noticeable in the soft light. It really was a disgraceful bit of underwear, no way to hide a freckle under material so revealing. When she pulled it over her head, the fabric was so cool and slinky on her bare skin that she shivered again.

The gown draped over her hips, then fell to the floor with a shimmering sound. She reached for the black lace peignoir to pull over it. As robes went, it didn't cover much, was never meant to cover much. A pair of satin strings held it together at the waist. Her fingers slipped, trying to tie it. Her hands were just so shaky.

The glare of headlights reflected in the window and seconds later, below, she heard the muffled sound of a car door slamming. Michael was already home.

Hurriedly she glanced around. She'd covered one of the steamer trunks with a scrap of Irish linen, creating a makeshift table. Two candles sat on top, red, set in art-deco sterling holders. The old wooden Victrola was already standing open. It had to be cranked to start, and the ancient records were red and cracked, old '78s. She'd picked out two from her grandmother's era. "Night and Day" and "Smoke Gets in Your Eyes."

Everything was ready. Everything that could be. Yet she walked to the top of the stairs and stopped, putting her hand to her stomach to quell the sick, dreadful feeling of nerves.

Michael could very well laugh if she tried to seduce him. Worse yet, he could be kind. Maybe Julia had the guts to dress this way for the man she loved, but Simone...she'd never had Julia's courage. She had no practice setting up candlelight-and-peignoir scenes. She'd never been one to take the kind of risks that could well end up in humiliation and embarrassment.

She took a long breath and closed her eyes.

When the kids had interrupted Michael from talking about Benjamin and Julia, she thought—believed—he'd been trying to express his feelings for her. But she wasn't sure. She wasn't at all sure. With his sons gone, he could have found a hundred ways to talk to her all day if he'd wanted to. He hadn't tried again.

Through a long anxiety-ridden day, she finally understood that the ball was in her court. If anything was going to happen, it was up to her to make it happen. Michael had already taken enormous risks for her. He'd been scarred by his divorce, she knew. He'd taken that failure personally, and yet he'd still opened his heart to her—a vulnerable man's heart, boundless in intuition and compassion and understanding where she was concerned.

And she'd never even tried to tell him how she felt. For the idiotic reason that she was afraid.

Her grandmother's diaries had already been shipped home to Colorado, yet the lovers' story had lingered in her mind all day. She'd been so sure, for so long, that their grandparents' affair was a telling lesson in heartbreak. The truth she discovered was that the older generation of lovers were simply two scarred people who found each other... and discovered a love so healing and powerful that it changed their lives.

Simone had always seen the similarities. She and Michael were scarred people, both afraid to risk loving again. Maybe it was logical that she was afraid of repeating the mistakes of the past. Her grandmother had lost the man she loved. The Hartman women had always lost the men they loved. Simone had lived out that same pattern with every man she'd been involved with.

But none of those other men had been Michael. And Simone wasn't Julia. Peignoirs and candlelight were terrifyingly flimsy weapons to fight with...but they were a way to lay her heart bare for Michael. Words were inadequate. She had to show him how she felt. There were painful, vulnerable risks she'd never taken for any man, risks she was willing to take with him...

If he wanted her.

Damn, but her heart was beating harder than a hiccuping horse and her hands were dripping nerves.

She squared her shoulders, sucked in a lungful of oxygen and called down the stairs, "Michael? Are you down there? Could you come up here for a minute?"

Thunder growled and boomed over the rocky shore. A drenching warm rain sluiced down the windows. Simone was still up in the attic, Michael knew.

He'd told her he was going to bring in take-out for their last dinner. He'd lied. He'd been out all right, and he'd brought in white cartons of Chinese to heat up for later, but that wasn't the only reason he'd taken a trip to town.

He struck a match, and lit the three white tapers on the table. The candles flickered and shone on the scarlet tablecloth, caught the glitter of the sterling silver icer. Lifting the bottle of champagne from the bed of ice, he twisted the cap. It blew, steam swirling out of the bottle.

He set two flute glasses on the table next to the single white camellia, then pulled on his jacket. The rented tux was black, the pleated shirt whiter than snow, and like all tuxes, was damnably uncomfortable to wear.

She could well laugh when she saw the corny setup, Michael thought gloomily. Worse yet, knowing Simone, she might be kind. She'd been kind before at his clumsy attempts to romance her. But he'd had an excuse then—understanding the old lovers—and that excuse wouldn't hold a lick of water now. They both knew how that story ended. The older lovers had failed.

Fear of failure had always been his personal nemesis. He never had, never could, easily walk into a situation where he felt inadequate. He'd learned the hard way to never take a woman's feelings for granted, and Simone had told him dozens of times that she had no use for anything as hoaxy and mawkishly sentimental as romance.

The candlelight and champagne were as hoaxily sentimental—and as subtle—as a freight train. Wearing the tux was heaping more risk on his head. Damned if he wasn't betting all his marbles on the insane gamble that he knew Simone...really knew her...maybe not at a logical mind level, but at the deeper level of emotions and heart. His intuition told him that she was soft at the core, but only afraid, terribly afraid, badly afraid, to expose that vulnerable side of her nature. If there was a key to winning her, it had to be by showing her that she was safe with him, that he was a man who would protect and value that softness.

He was sure of that—in theory. His instincts had failed him before, though, and the whole history of Connor men with women had painfully ingrained caution about stupidly trusting his heart. None of them knew how to love a woman. The story of the old lovers had first swayed Michael into believing that Benjamin was different, but that proved false. Old Ben had been a maestro wooer, but ultimately he'd lost the only woman he ever loved.

Michael didn't like that ending.

Echoes of the past had haunted him before, but never more than tonight. The history lesson was painfully clear. Benjamin had let the woman of his heart go without a fight. Michael had no intention of making that mistake.

But damned if he wasn't scared straight to the pit of his belly.

Before he could change his mind, he doused the candles, grabbed the camellia and heaved in a lungful of oxygen for courage. Lightning crackled and thunder boomed as he strode toward the foot of the stairs. "Simone? Are you up there? Could you come down for a minute?"

"Michael?" Simone called his name again and then rolled her eyes in embarrassing frustration. For heaven's sake, she was three floors up. He couldn't possibly hear her over the growly noise of the thunderstorm.

Lifting the gown, she pelted barefoot down the attic stairs...and then stopped dead when she saw the shadow in the doorway.

A ghost couldn't have startled her more. For an instant she actually thought he was Benjamin. The elegant tux, the old-world courtly posture, the handsome, shadowed face with the haunted eyes...she'd imagined Benjamin looking like this, dressed to romance his lover, frozen in time, a man forever searching for the love he'd lost.

But then she saw the camellia in his hand. This was no Benjamin, no ghost, no stranger. He was twisting the stem on the fragile white flower—only Michael would be dying of nerves around a woman. His Adam's apple thumped down a swallow. Only Michael could manage to convey acute anxiety in such a small gesture. His eyes met hers only for the whisk of a second, but even in the dim light of the stairwell, she caught the luminous sheen of raw fear in his eyes. Only Michael would automatically assume a rejection. Michael was always going to assume a woman would reject him.

But he was still here. Her heart started beating. Slowly, softly, haltingly, as if every pulse of a beat was precious and she couldn't catch her breath. Maybe she didn't care if she ever caught her breath again. He really was still here . . . and taking his worst nemesis of a risk. For her.

His gaze traveled the length of her with the same memorizing intensity as she did him. He took in the red satin gown and black lace peignoir. He took in her bare feet. He watched her swallow and he noticed her shaky hands and, Michael being Michael, he probably noticed the huge well of hope in her eyes. She'd never managed to hide her feelings. Not from him. And slowly, he smiled. That roguish, quiet-man smile that was uniquely Michael's.

"Ah . . . Simone?"

"Hmm?"

"I'm getting the feeling that we're on the same wavelength."

She nodded. Any second her vocal cords were going to function. Just then she couldn't get a word past the huge, welling lump of emotion in her throat to save her life.

"I don't know why I'm surprised. You and I have been on the same wavelength from the day we met. You always seemed to know what I was feeling. I never had that kind of connection with another human being. Until you. Only with you."

Simone had always felt that kindred spirit connection, but this was more. It was still sinking in, that the fear in his eyes mirrored her own. That he'd chosen the exact same symbols to express his heart as she had. Need. She needed him like her heart's breath, but until that moment had never believed that he needed her, too. How could Michael possibly be afraid of *her*? She thought he knew. If not, she'd take a lifetime to teach him. There was no mountain she wouldn't cross with him, nothing he couldn't say, no problem he had to hide. There was nothing he could fail at. Not with her.

She took the first step... and then launched into his arms.

Michael, startled almost to laughter, caught her in an exuberant swing. She pinned his ears, trying to pull his head down for a kiss. She didn't have to pull hard. His mouth sought hers, found hers, and shared the beginning of a kiss that started out joyful and wild... and ended up in a slow, soaring-soft, spinning dip of emotion. He had the brief, terrifying thought that she was always going to do this to him. Bewilder him, with the sheer bursting power of love he felt for her.

He let her up for air. Not too much air. And not for long. "I love you," he whispered. "I almost went crazy, thinking you were going to leave. Thinking I was going to have to live without you. Thinking there wasn't a way in hell you could love me."

"I thought you knew." The look in her eyes was as soft as a hush and smoky with emotion. "I fell scared witless in love with you almost from the day we met. I was just so frightened, Michael. I'd watched every woman in my family gamble on want-to-believe and fairy-tale romances. And lose. I didn't trust what I felt. I didn't believe it."

"I was never pretending at romance. I was never playing with you. Everything I felt for you was real. I just didn't know how to make you believe it." His hands cupped her shoulders, slid slowly, possessively over satin and lace. His voice turned husky. "You're starting to believe, though, aren't you? You're dressed awfully slinky for you, Ms. Hartman."

There. He won a smile. "I dressed for my lover," she said honestly. "I didn't know how else to show you what I felt. I'm always going to be realistic and pragmatic, Michael. I think a woman has to be practical to be strong in life.... But it's not the way I want to be with the man I love. It's not how I want to be with you."

"I know," he murmured, "exactly how pragmatic and realistic you are. I wouldn't have you any other way."

The attic door clicked shut behind them with the unmistakable sound of a lock turning. Michael paid no attention. It wasn't as if either of them were immediately going downstairs. The candlelit dinner would wait. He couldn't.

He stole a kiss before swooping up his practical, realistic lover and spiriting her up the stairs. She was kissing him back so hard, so blindly and completely, that he darn near risked dropping her. Only not really.

He wasn't about to lose Simone. He wasn't about to repeat any of the mistakes the Connor men had made in the past. Michael turned the corner on the attic stairs, thinking that he wanted her last name changed quickly; he wanted her children; he wanted her irreversibly part of his life and all the ties that bound. He wanted the right to dance in the moonlight with her when they were both a hundred and ten.

And from the radiance in her eyes, from the fire and emotion in her kisses, he knew damn well that Simone had the same realistic goals in mind.

Epilogue

Lar, what a wedding. Jock had never seen such mass confusion in his entire life—and his life span had been considerable. The minister had conducted the service from the rocky jut of land by the lighthouse. The fall wind nipping off the ocean had lifted all the lasses' skirts. Zachary had played the wedding march on a tenor sax. It was the sexiest wedding march, for sure, that Jock had ever heard. Simone had worn a traditional white gown with lace trim and a train. Her veil whipped all over the place in the breeze, and there wasn't a soul who understood why she carried a bouquet of mixed camellias and four-leaf clovers—except for the lovers. And, of course, him.

Jock leaned over the windowsill with a deep sigh of satisfaction. The ties were bound, the rituals over. But the madcap of a party was still picking up steam. Wedding or not, the three brothers had made up their minds they were going to barbecue steaks for the guests—and in this wind. Kirstin's daughter and Michael's young sons were whooping and screaming around the rocks, looking for frogs—in their good clothes yet!—and trailed by a behemoth of a big black Newfoundland bounding after them. Jock remembered that unmanageable beast all too well.

Zach and Kirstin's new baby was snoozing in a cradle in the yard. Seth's wife, Samantha, checked to make sure the little one was still covered about every three minutes or so. Her fascination with the tyke was understandable. Samantha's stomach was blooming. A bun in her own oven for sure. The whole clan of Connor women were adding to the confusion. The lasses were carting out platters of food from the house, setting up the feast on tables outside and prattling ten for a dozen the whole time. Jock had no way to keep track of the women. Nor was he trying.

It was the Connor men's conversation that had him captivated . . . and chortling.

Michael was attempting to light the grill for the third time. Zach and Seth were offering lots of advice. The brothers hadn't had a moment alone until now. Seth, typically, had shorn his tux jacket as soon as the ceremony was over. "I have to admit, I'm glad you kept the house. I think all of us developed a certain attachment for the old monster."

"I'll be stuck with some commuting for a while. I found a manager for the plants, but he's still wet behind the ears." Michael ruefully shook his head. "Simone's already found a dozen business ventures around here for me to look into. She doesn't want me changing my mind about keeping it."

Zach said casually, "You never owned up."

"Owned up about what?"

"About whether you heard all the legends about the ghost."

"Jock?" Michael lifted his head and grinned. "Sure, we heard the stories. And don't go kidding her about it, but I think Simone halfway—at least a little—believes he's real."

"I'm glad you admitted it first, because Samantha bought into the idea hook, line and sinker."

"Kirstin, too," Zach admitted, and then rolled his eyes. "Women! But hell, I didn't argue with her. I never could change that woman's mind about anything, anyway. And if she gets a charge out of believing the house is haunted, what's the harm?"

"That's exactly the attitude I took," Seth agreed. "Samantha gets a real kick out of psychic lore. I just indulge her. So she's real tickled by this Jock ghost— doesn't bother me as long as she isn't hurt by it."

"We know the reality," Michael said.

"Exactly," Seth said firmly.

"You bet," Zach agreed.

Jock had to muffle an outright laugh. None of the brothers were looking at each other. None of them probably dared.

"Michael!"

Jock craned his head to catch a view of the bride. Simone's voice had the landmark ring of a feminine imperial summons. She wanted her lover and she wanted him now. Michael, innocent new husband that he was, went running.

Momentarily Jock fretted that the lad was going to turn out henpecked—there was *nothing* Michael wouldn't do to please that lass—but his behavior proved reassuring. Simone was standing on the porch steps, her white dress whipping around her ankles, and she was surely frustrated about something—some plate she couldn't reach or some dadblame thing like that. Michael came at her beck and call, all right, but she never had a chance to vent that frustration. He swooped her up, and as fast as the snap of a sail, layered her flat against the porch wall. They were out of sight then. All Jock heard after that was "hmm" and "Oh, Michael!" and then "ummm" again.

Jock pulled back from the window with a yawn. All was as it should be. For the first time in nigh two centuries, he could finally rest. Of all the lovers he'd helped over the years, truly the Connor brothers touched him the most. The lads had known far too much unhappiness. They'd presented some exhausting challenges but thankfully—as Jock knew well—the strongest man born was still and always vulnerable to the right woman.

It nipped a tad that the lads had denied him credit, but hells bells. Jock knew the truth. The boys had all found true loves . . . solely, of course, because of his help.

*   *   *   *   *

CAN YOU STAND THE HEAT?

Silhouette™
SUMMER
Sizzlers '94

You're in for a serious heat wave with
Silhouette's latest selection of sizzling
summer reading. This sensuous collection
of three short stories provides the perfect
vacation escape! And what better authors
to relax with than

ANNETTE BROADRICK
JACKIE MERRITT
JUSTINE DAVIS

And that's not all....

With the purchase of *Silhouette Summer
Sizzlers '94*, you can send in for a FREE
Summer Sizzlers beach bag!

SUMMER JUST GOT HOTTER—
WITH SILHOUETTE BOOKS!

Take 4 bestselling love stories FREE

Plus get a FREE surprise gift!

Special Limited-time Offer

Mail to Silhouette Reader Service™

3010 Walden Avenue
P.O. Box 1867
Buffalo, N.Y. 14269-1867

YES! Please send me 4 free Silhouette Desire® novels and my free surprise gift. Then send me 6 brand-new novels every month, which I will receive months before they appear in bookstores. Bill me at the low price of $2.44 each plus 25¢ delivery and applicable sales tax, if any.* That's the complete price and—compared to the cover prices of $2.99 each—quite a bargain! I understand that accepting the books and gift places me under no obligation ever to buy any books. I can always return a shipment and cancel at any time. Even if I never buy another book from Silhouette, the 4 free books and the surprise gift are mine to keep forever.

225 BPA ANRS

Name	(PLEASE PRINT)	
Address		Apt. No.
City	State	Zip

This offer is limited to one order per household and not valid to present Silhouette Desire® subscribers. *Terms and prices are subject to change without notice.
Sales tax applicable in N.Y.

UDES-94R ©1990 Harlequin Enterprises Limited

**Rugged and lean...and the best-looking,
sweetest-talking men to be found in the
entire Lone Star state!**

*Diana
Palmer*

**LONG, TALL
TEXANS**

In July 1994, Silhouette is very proud to bring you
Diana Palmer's first three LONG, TALL TEXANS.
CALHOUN, JUSTIN and TYLER—the three cowboys
who started the legend. Now they're back by popular
demand in one classic volume—and they're ready to
lasso your heart! Beautifully repackaged for this
special event, this collection is sure to be a
longtime keepsake!

"Diana Palmer makes a reader want to find a Texan
of her own to love!"   —*Affaire de Coeur*

**LONG, TALL TEXANS—the first three—
reunited in this special roundup!**

**Available in July,
wherever Silhouette books are sold.**

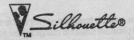

LTT

SILHOUETTE®

Desire®

**They're sexy, they're determined, they're trouble
with a capital *T*!**

Meet six of the steamiest, most stubborn heroes you'd ever
want to know, and learn *everything* about them....

August's *Man of the Month,* Quinn Donovan, in
FUSION by Cait London

Mr. Bad Timing, Dan Kingman, in
DREAMS AND SCHEMES by Merline Lovelace

Mr. Marriage-phobic, Connor Devlin, in
WHAT ARE FRIENDS FOR? by Naomi Horton

Mr. Sensible, Lucas McCall, in **HOT PROPERTY**
by Rita Rainville

Mr. Know-it-all, Thomas Kane, in **NIGHTFIRE**
by Barbara McCauley

Mr. Macho, Jake Powers, in **LOVE POWER**
by Susan Carroll

Look for them on the covers so you can see just how
handsome and irresistible they are!

Coming in August only from Silhouette Desire!   CENTER

IT'S OUR 1000TH SILHOUETTE ROMANCE, AND WE'RE CELEBRATING!

JOIN US FOR A SPECIAL COLLECTION OF LOVE STORIES BY AUTHORS YOU'VE LOVED FOR YEARS, AND NEW FAVORITES YOU'VE JUST DISCOVERED. JOIN THE CELEBRATION...

April
REGAN'S PRIDE by Diana Palmer
MARRY ME AGAIN by Suzanne Carey

May
THE BEST IS YET TO BE by Tracy Sinclair
CAUTION: BABY AHEAD by Marie Ferrarella

June
THE BACHELOR PRINCE by Debbie Macomber
A ROGUE'S HEART by Laurie Paige

July
IMPROMPTU BRIDE by Annette Broadrick
THE FORGOTTEN HUSBAND by Elizabeth August

SILHOUETTE ROMANCE...VIBRANT, FUN AND EMOTIONALLY RICH! TAKE ANOTHER LOOK AT US! AND AS PART OF THE CELEBRATION, READERS CAN RECEIVE A FREE GIFT!

**YOU'LL FALL IN LOVE ALL OVER
AGAIN WITH
SILHOUETTE ROMANCE!**

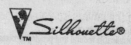

CEL1000

Coming Next Month from

SILHOUETTE®

Desire®

The next in the delightful

HAZARDS, INC.

series

THE PIRATE PRINCESS
BY
SUZANNE SIMMS

When Nick decides to take some vacation time on Key West, he never expects to get mixed up in Melina Morgan's zany plans to find her ancestor's long-lost buried treasure!

HAZARDS, INC.: Danger is their business; love is their reward!

SILHOUETTE®

Desire®

Big Bad **WOLFE**

WOLFE WATCHING
by Joan Hohl

Undercover cop Eric Wolfe knew *everything* about divorcée Tina Kranas, from her bra size to her bedtime—without ever having spent the night with her! The lady was a suspect, and Eric had to keep a close eye on her. But since his binoculars were getting all steamed up from watching her, Eric knew it was time to start wooing her....

WOLFE WATCHING, Book 2 of Joan Hohl's devilishly sexy Big Bad Wolfe series, is coming your way in July...only from Silhouette Desire.